The Old Woman Who Refused to Die

Stories and Tales by
Sarah Udoh-Grossfurthner

*To Divami, Enjoy my,
friendship... I Love...*

ISBN: 978-3-9503433-4-2
Cover art by: Barbara Prešinskă

The beginning of wisdom is this: Get Wisdom.
Though it cost all you have, get understanding:

Proverb 4:7 The Holy Bible,
New International Version

Acknowledgement

A proverb of my region states, 'One rich in money has only a small portion of wealth, but a person who is rich in people owns all aspects of wealth.' That you are holding a copy of this book is by the grace of all the people in my life who love, support and believe in me. Together, the support system they give made the realization of *The Old Woman Who Refused to Die* possible. And so with the deepest gratitude, I acknowledge:

- my amazing children, Stefan and Nina. My dearest mother, Ima Akpan Udoh-Akpan Amaetor. Mama, brothers, sisters and other family members.
- my dearest friends, and all who believe in my me and my work – you know who you are because you donated to support this project during its crowdfunding stage.
- my editor, Brian Gresko, also a writer.
- my proofreader, Catherine Evans (publisher & editor, www. pennyshorts.com)
- the elders, those wise men and women, of my community who taught me the art and craft of story-telling.
- most importantly, my gratitude to God for giving me the power and the ability to will, and to do.

I am truly grateful
Sarah Udoh-Grossfurthner, Vienna, 2019

Table of Contents

Introduction

My life began on a farm. The high point of each day was the evening when the moon was out, after we had eaten and cleared everything away. That was when the members of our community, young and old, gathered around the big baobab tree in the village square for the day's round of storytelling.

Each story began and ended with the storyteller chanting 'Ekong nke-e', to which the listeners responded,

'Nke ekong Abasi. Ekong aka, ekong oyong, ekong isi maha udim.'

Or simply,

'Nke ekong Abasi.'

At the end of each moon cycle, when the evenings became dark, the sprawling woodland and forests became foreboding, so the storytelling evenings continued in each individual family's compound, inside their efe. An efe was a half-walled construction of clay and earth, finished with charcoal and iduot, a red local coloring agent also used for skincare. The smoothed walls were decorated on the outside with sea or cowrie shells, while the insides were lined with drawings of wildlife in clay and charcoal. The roof was traditionally laid with palm fronds, but the richer folk roofed theirs with zinc and completed the walls with cement. An efe was where the patriarch of the family received his guests.

Every now and then, stories were told by young people and children, but the floor usually belonged to the elders, 'the wise' of the land. Story-telling time was an opportunity to relax after the grueling labor of the day. It was highly prized as a chance to entertain and be entertained, but there was one aspect to it that everyone, even children, understood from the very beginning; it was an opportunity to learn. And who better to learn from than from the elders, those whom the whole community saw as the custodians of our history?

A popular saying of my community states, 'the lamp is the present, the wicker is the future, and the past is the light that ignites the wicker.' Without the light, both the lamp and the wicker are useless.

In Akwa Ibom State, the region in Nigeria where I was born and partly raised, we regarded the elders as that light. They were the knowledge-keepers, our rural community's equivalent to the libraries in the urban cities. For that reason, younger people were never in a hurry to jump in with our stories in place of theirs. And so, while these old men and women serenaded us with stories of love and hate, of loss and redemption, while they told us cautionary and captivating tales, we sat, spellbound, as still as lions about to pounce. Legs crossed, and with rapt attention. It was storytelling time. It was handing over time.

That was more than thirty years ago. I am no longer a child but rather, a grown woman, who is slowly edging towards her own twilight years. Though I am not sitting under the imposing baobab of my childhood, it is my turn to carry on the revered tradition of my people... the handing over of what we believe in, through the art of storytelling. So, thank you for picking up *The Old Woman Who Refused to Die*.

Ekong nke-e...

Sarah Udoh-Grossfurthner, Vienna, 2018
(With the deepest gratitude to those who came before me)

2

The Old Woman Who Refused to Die

ESIT-IMA Samson comes out of the main house in time to hear an old transistor radio warble out the end of the hourly news. The noise was coming from the efe, the opened thatched hut next to the family's main house, where her father receives his visitors. Balancing a silver enameled tray, atop which sits a container full of a light grey liquid and a jar labelled Vaseline, Esit-Ima makes her way slowly towards the hut. It is the harmattan season, a period known for its dramatic cool air during the early mornings, and intense dry heat during the day. It is now late afternoon. The efe is built under a big baobab tree. It is an imposing tree, with roots and sinews crisscrossing in and out the ground around the efe. The branches of the giant tree tower above the hut, spreading their leaves over the hall in a manner that reminds Esit-Ima of a photo she had once seen of the Pope, spreading his hands over a large crowd in benediction. Esit-Ima has since come to compare the giant baobab tree in their home to the Pope, and all who sit in the efe as the congregation.

As Esit-Ima makes her way forward, a leaf falls from the tree, landing right on the tray. She stops, lowers her face directly above it, puffs her lips, and blows. The leaf lifts and sails out of the tray. It lands right in front of her and she steps on it. The dry

3

leaf crackles under her feet. Esit-Ima looks up the tree as if to apologize for stepping on what could essentially be called a part of its body. A gust of wind blows at that particular moment and the branches shake and weave, disgorging more leaves onto the tray. She bends her head forward again to blow away the leaves. Once more, she looks up at the tree, smiling and shaking her head as she does so. Then she resumes walking and enters the hut. The place smells tangy and cool, definitely cooler than the inside of the main house, which is built of zinc and cement. The inside walls are lined with long benches made from bamboo. But neither her father nor any visitor is present in the efe at the moment. Only a lone, stooped figure sits inside. And she isn't sitting on a bench, but cross-legged in the centre of the hall, on a raffia mat. Her back is supported by two large cow-skin futons, gifts from Esit-Ima's fiancé, who brought them from northern Nigeria on his last work visit there. Esit-Ima smiles fondly as she advances towards the stooped figure.

It is her grandmother. Everyone calls the old woman Ekamba-Ma – Big Mother – or Nne; but to Esit-Ima, she is Nana. Nana was the first-word Esit-Ima uttered as a toddler.

'Nana,' Esit-Ima coos now, balancing the tray carefully as she walks in.

The old woman looks up. Her mouth breaks into a wide grin. Most of her teeth are gone.

Her Nana had been a beauty in her day, with light brown skin, thick, dark brown woolly hair, and deep hazel eyes. Nana had told her that when she was a girl, the men who courted her said those eyes were as sparkling as a tiger's. The same suitors told her that her teeth were like waterfalls glittering on a hot sunny day.

'My teeth were that white,' her Nana mused. 'Age is a beautiful thing, my heart. It is a clear sign that the heavens have blessed you with long life. But, it can mock you without mercy when you stand in front of a mirror during your twilight years.'

The signs of Nana's famed beauty are rare and flitting, like the faded imprint of a disappearing rainbow. The thick, woolly brown hair, though still full, is now white and fluffy, like the cotton candy Esit-Ima once tasted at a birthday party as a child. The smooth, light-toned skin is tight and dry, and craggy lines run from the edge of her cheeks and disappear into her hairline like the ridges on a badly tarred road. Long ago, her grandmother had had a beauty tattoo stenciled at the corner of those same eyes and on the bottom of her chin – a tiny star-like shape, reminiscent of a star anise seed.

'They used to draw attention to my cat's eyes and my waterfall teeth,' the old woman told Esit-Ima many times, smiling coquettishly. The shape of the tattoos is formless now, and the one on her chin no longer visible as her lower lips had caved in. The rheumy eyes now peer owlishly at Esit-Ima from behind thick lenses. 'Koko-nmi,' Nana calls out to Esit-Ima.

Esit-Ima's smiles. *Koko-nmi* means 'my namesake'. Her Nana had given her the formal name Esit-Ima, Love-Heart, but usually called her 'my heart' or 'my heartbeat.'

The old woman beckons Esit-Ima forward with a wiry hand. 'Come! Sit!' The hand is dry and wrinkly as the rest of her; the fingers are like the claws on a giant spider.

Age. Every part of her beloved Nana is riddled with signs of it. It makes Esit-Ima fearful, as her Nana's days on earth are numbering fewer. She will not always be around. She loves the old woman more than anyone else in the world.

Some say her Nana is ninety years old, others say more like a hundred, or a hundred-and-ten. No one knows her real age. Esit-Ima's father is fifty-four years old. He is the youngest of her Nana's nine children.

The old woman always dresses in *Up and Down*, a two-piece outfit traditionally made with a colourful fabric, or *a tie-and-die* adire material. It is a large wrap and loose-sleeved blouse. Today, her grandmother's Up and Down is a brown tie-dye with white circular designs. The outfit overwhelms her grandmother in folds and swaps, as if made for a much larger person.

'Come sit,' her Nana commands again, patting a space beside her on the mat. 'It does my heart good to see you, my beloved; but shouldn't you be preparing for your upcoming nuptials?'

'Oh, pssph! That can wait, Nana. Besides, there's a week to go before the Visit of Intent, six before the formal acceptance, and eight before the actual marriage.'

'And all of them involve lots of preparations and planning,' Nana insists.

'I know, Nana. Oh, don't I know!' Esit-Ima harrumphs in mock exhaustion as she lowers the jug of grey liquid onto one corner of the mat. 'Why are you in a rush to get rid of me, anyway? Who will prepare your favourite drink when I'm gone? Tell me that, you beautiful but naughty old woman.' Esit-Ima leans forward, wraps her arms around the old woman and gives her a stiff embrace.

'Hey! Hey! Careful, child, unless you wish to break all the remaining bones in this wrinkly old bag I call a body,' the old woman pushes her away playfully. She giggles.

'Oh, come, you are the most beautiful girl here and you know it.'

'Beautiful girl? Didn't you just call me old a few seconds ago?'

'If I were a man and not your granddaughter,' Esit-Ima continues unabated, 'I would propose to you right here and right now. I would be on my hands and knees, begging, pleading, kissing.' So saying, Esit-Ima plants a loud wet kiss on her grand-mother's craggy forehead.

'Oh, shush, you! Keep your saliva where it belongs...in your mouth,' the old woman continues to giggle as she takes one end of her wrapper and rigorously wipes the forehead her grand-daughter has just kissed.

'So, what were you listening to just before I came in? I heard the news,' Esit-Ima says, pointing to the radio which never leaves her grandmother's side.

They say her grandmother bought her first radio with the money she saved selling gathered palm nuts. The story of her Nana's radio was the first story Esit-Ima had ever learned.

Her Nana had been one of the wives of the local Chief at the time. The Chief himself had married her to prove he was the only man who could break the 'spirited' Uwa-Nne Ituen. At a time when most young girls were married off by the time they were seventeen years old, and had three or four children by the age of twenty-five, Nana had been single still at twenty-four. Despite her jaw-dropping beauty, no man wanted to marry elder Ituen's 'mouthy' daughter. Most prospective suitors were intimidated by the young girl 'who did not hesitate to offer her opinions liberally,' even in the presence of men. Older men too, for that matter, something that was frowned upon as 'not befitting a well-brought-up girl from a good home.'

7

'They used to say I was the kind of girl who would not hesitate to slap her husband right back if he dared to lay his hand on me,' Nana once told Esit-Ima with a devilish glint in her eyes. 'They were right, though I never had to do it.'

Esit-Ima grew up knowing that in a society where men feel they can lord it over women, her Nana was a woman that no one messed with. Not even Esit-Ima's grandpa, who passed away before she was born, had dared to raise his hand to his 'wilful' wife. Her Nana was not only unafraid to speak her mind, she was also known to be intensely curious, with a burning wish to learn and acquire knowledge, something that was considered an extremely strange trait in a woman.

'They used to say that I knew too much, that I sought to know things a woman had no right to know. They were not pleased when I bought my radio.'

Despite their disapproval at her outspokenness, there was something everyone, including her most ardent critics, agreed on... Uwa-Nne Ituen was a woman of the highest integrity, the kind of woman who was prepared to 'have a noose wrapped around her neck' for something she believed in. She was also kindhearted, and would not hesitate to 'give you the last wrap around her waist' if you were in need and it was all she had to give. It was one of the reasons she became, and remains, the sole female on the Council of Chiefs, a body that lays down the rules and laws that govern their community. Nana had been awarded this honour on her seventy-fifth birthday.

Five years after her marriage to the Chief, Esit-Ima's grandfather, she was still unable to conceive. Amidst whisperings and finger-pointing, and the Chief's subsequent marriage to two more wives, Nana had decided to find comfort and solace in a new invention that was making the rounds in the homes of those who could afford it. The invention was popularly called 'The Talking Box.' It brought news from as far afield as Lagos, and from the land of the 'pale skins,' a place Nana quickly learned was called Europe.

'It was the most wondrous thing our rural community had ever beheld, my heart,' Nana told Esit-Ima. 'But it was an invention only the very wealthy could afford. At that time they said the money needed to buy this incredible thing could build an entire hut for a family of six! Anyone who spent such a vast sum on a tiny, albeit wondrous, thing like the Talking Box was looked at with respect and unconcealed envy.

'Having been all but ignored and relegated as "insignificant and useless" because of my inability to conceive, I decided I was going to buy such a box. It was going to be my consolation for the one thing the world had refused to give me, that which completes a woman... a child.'

They say the Chief's family was aghast when his 'barren, headstrong' wife bought the Talking Box, more so because she hadn't asked her husband's permission before doing so. They demanded that she be 'disciplined' for such a 'show of disrespect.' Knowing his wife as he did, the Chief was reluctant to punish her in the way that his friends, family and Council of Chiefs demanded, but he did decree that Nana pay a fine in the form of a live he-goat and a five-liter jug of akaikai, the locally-brewed gin. Which Nana did.

'And gladly, my heart. I wasn't going to let anything get between me and my magical Box.'

The Talking Box became Nana's constant companion. Soon, people knew she was around a particular area just by listening for the sound of the radio. Even when she worked on the farm it was to be found nestling protectively in a bed of old clothing.

'I didn't want to risk it getting damaged. In those days, no one could repair such a thing. Once it was broken you had to buy a new one. I had barely been able to afford the first one.'

Nana treated her radio with so much love that most came to view it as her child. Because it is the custom of our region for people to call women after the name of their first child, especially if that child is male, it wasn't long before the community and all who knew Uwa-Nne Ituen took to calling her Eka Udedio (Radio's mother).

Barely six months after getting the radio she became pregnant. She subsequently gave birth to a boy. As male children were highly favoured, her status in the Samson family was instantly restored. In the next ten years, Nana gave birth to five more boys and two girls, cementing her position in the Chief's home. But her love for her magic box remained strong.

'How could it not, dear child? This invention had brought me luck. It opened my closed womb, not to mention the fact that it also filled my head with knowledge of so many things I had never before imagined. It was through that radio that I learned that someone named Hitler was building fire camps to kill all the Jews in a country called Germany. It was also through that radio that our community learned of the big, big war that came about because of the terrible deeds that man was doing. I learned of a man named Gandhi, from a place named India, who was trying to bring freedom to his people without raising a single sword. I learned of black people in the 'American South' being treated worse than vagrant dogs on the street. I learned about Nkrumah. And in our own country, I learned about Zik. And of course oil then called black gold. I learned of Fumilayo Kuti and Margaret Ekpo, fighting for the rights of women. What I learned, my heart, that the world wasn't filled only with war and destruction and hatred. I learned of a man name named Babe Ruth, playing a strange game called baseball. I learned how this man was taking a whole region called America 'by storm' because of his supernatural knowledge of this game. I learned of a man called Armstrong who landed on the moon. Imagine that, my heart, sitting in this small community of ours and learning that in a world out there, far, far away, that a wondrous thing like that was taking place! I learned things, Koko-nmi. I learned things. And that knowledge made people look at me with distrust. And maybe a little fear, who will ever know?'

That was more than seventy years ago. That first old transistor radio still occupied the pride of place in her Nana's bedroom even though it had long ceased to work. Over the years, many radios had come and gone, but each was treated by her Nana with as much care as the first.

'Tell me, Nana! What new madness is going on in the world?' asked Esit-Ima, as she lays her head gently on the old woman's fragile shoulder.

The old woman pats her gently. 'Mmmh,' she says 'this terrible day-in, day-out suicide bombing in the Nod, that's what.' *Nod* was her term for the North. 'I'll tell you all about it in a moment.' Pointing at the tray Esit-Ima had brought she says, 'First, pass me the jug, please.' Esit-Ima obeys. Her Nana takes a sip, gulps, and hurriedly puts down the jug, squeezing her wrinkled face in a comical, child-like way.

'What's wrong? Don't you like it?'

'Rather strong, this juice today, my heart. Very gingery.'

'Gingery? But you like it that way, Nana. You always say to put in more ginger than coconut water and lemongrass.'

'Yes, but proportion, my heart. Proportion is the keyword. This drink of yours today almost pulled out my tongue from its root.'

'I am sorry, Nana. Should I go and make another?' Esit-Ima's tone is woebegone as she struggles to get up.

'No. Never mind. A bit of variation never killed anyone.' So saying, the old woman picks up the jug and takes another tentative sip. Then putting it down, she turns to Esit-Ima. 'Now, where were we?'

'You were going to tell me the latest news, about the suicide bombing in the North. But first, your foot massage.' Esit-Ima picks up the jar marked Vaseline. She pops open the container. It does not contain Vaseline. Instead, the content is a brown viscous liquid. Esit-Ima takes a dollop of runny liquid between two fingers. 'Let's hope my massage today will be better than the juice I have made.'

The old woman giggles as she stretches forth both legs and pulls her wrap away from them. Esit-Ima lathers the wiry legs with the lotion and begins to massage the old woman.

The old woman watches her for a few seconds, then she lifts up her left hand and caresses Esit-Ima's head. 'You are a good child, a tender child. Your young man, he has found himself a priceless treasure,' she says.

'Esit- Ima looks up and smiles. 'You can tell me the story as I work, Nana,' she says.

'Ah, yes, the suicide bombing. Twenty-three people killed this time in Maiduguri. And they used a child-bomber this time. An innocent child... they are using young children. Young, innocent children! What a world we live in,' Nana lowers her head and shakes it back and forth.

'That is terrible, Nana. I can't understand why a mother, a mother who has suffered through pregnancy and the agony of labour would keep quiet and allow her child to be used as a suicide bomber!'

'My child...'

'These people!' Esit-Ima stops the massage for a moment. 'What kind of people are these? And all in the name of a so-called religion! I'd rather be without religion than be a part of one that butchers and kills innocent people!'

'Shsssh!!! Don't speak that way, my heart. This, what is happening, is not the fault of the religion. It is the fault of the selfish, power-mad men responsible for these terrible deeds. They want power by all means and will kill and destroy everything standing in their path to get it. Religion has n...'

'True, Nana, but they are doing so under the name of their religion.'

'It still doesn't make it the fault of the religion.'

'And the mothers of these children,' Esit-Ima continues, unfazed by her Nana's tone, 'how can they support such madness? What kind of women are these? Giving up their children to be used for such? Better that their kind is barren, never able to conceive!'

'Hai! Child, how you talk! Do not!'

'But, Nana, it's...'

'I say, shsssh! Shush, my heart. There are many things you do not understand. Many, many things. I do believe that the time has come for me to tell you a story. A story of a different kind than the old ones I have shared with you and your cousins. You are a university-going girl of twenty-three. And you're about to embark on your own life path. I don't think you should do so without a certain understanding. So, listen. Listen attentively to my stories, and learn from them.'

'*Ekong nke-e,*' Nana chants. And Esit-Ima lowers her face in contrition and responds quietly, '*Nke ekong Abasi. Ekong aka, ekong oyong, ekong isi maha udim...*'

The White Abaya

Moments after the blast, a fragment of stained, white fabric rose from the rubble. Limp and forlorn, it fluttered for a second in mid-air before rising up again.

Up and up, the lone piece of abaya climbed alongside the red-spattered pole, where it was snagged, eventually, by the mangled remains of the electric wire.

And there it came to rest, along with other unidentifiable debris.

xx

HER stomach was cramping again. And it was hot...so hot!

A good day to splash around in the river. I'll there later with Kabir, Falmata thought, but then she remembered; that wasn't going to be possible. Today was the special day. The day that she, 'a simple girl, a common girl,' had been chosen to do something extraordinary for Allah, Alhaji Gambo, her uncle, had said. The thought took her focus away from the heat for a moment. Her hands shook. Falmata looked over quickly at the two men in the back of the truck with her. Malam Zarami, her uncle's right-hand man, and the Silent One. Neither of them seemed to notice her nervousness. Quickly, Falmata shoved her shaking hands under the folds of the grey shawl covering her head and upper body.

'And just think, when you arrive in heaven, you get to be welcomed by Allah himself and his most revered prophet, Mohammad...peace be upon him,' her uncle had said. 'What honour! What a privilege!' His fingers had flicked rapidly across the prayer beads wrapped permanently around his right wrist. 'And remember. Be still. No sudden movement until the appointed time. Pay attention!'

Falmata hoped she would remember all his instructions. He will get so angry if I don't, and then he'll take it out on Ma'a. This was exactly what had happened when she was first told of her mission. She had been so afraid, especially when she realized that accomplishing the mission would mean never again seeing her family. Never again seeing her mother. The thought had caused her to trip over her words and mix up the instructions – delivered daily by Uncle Gambo.

Falmata shifted uncomfortably again in her seat. She was squashed between the two men and the folds of their flowing kaftans seemed to intensify the heat. Perspiration trickled down her back. The vehicle bucked and swayed, plunging into every pothole and crevice along the seemingly endless road.

The two goats in the truck were feeling the heat, too. They bleated pitifully every now and then. It had been Malam Zarami's idea to bring them along with the calabash of freshly prepared Fura da nono – the dry season's popular millet and hibiscus flower drink. It was the Khari weekly market day in Maiduguri town. He'd suggested that they were less likely to be disturbed by soldiers manning the checkpoints along the way if their journey could be attributed to the market. The checkpoints were many: their truck was barely through with one roadblock before another materialized around the next corner of the main road leading to the centre of the city. Falmata heard Malam Zarami inform his silent companion that it had been that way since the spate of bombing had begun six months before. 'But their meddling cannot stop us,' her uncle's right-hand man grumbled under his breath each time their truck was brought to a stop by another line of soldiers in army uniforms.

'Remember, Yaa'na,' Ma'a had whispered tenderly last night, as she cuddled Falmata, 'Allah is with you. You're doing this for him; so he'll take care of you. Just concentrate on that thought.'

'Ma'a?' Falmata had whispered back as she burrowed into the warm, musky smell of her mother's bosom.

'Yes, Yaa'na?'

'Is it really what Allah wants… for me to go on this journey?'

Her mother was silent for what seemed a very long time. Just when Falmata thought she wasn't going to get an answer, her mother exhaled deeply.

'Everything that happens is the will of Allah.' A faraway look had come to her mother's face. Falmata saw the momentary confusion, but it was just that, momentary. And then, as if her mother too needed convincing, she had added 'Eh,' before snuggling Falmata some more.

Her mother didn't usually share Falmata's sleeping pallet. Girls were encouraged from a young age to sleep alone, or share sleeping pallets with other girls in the family. Since most were married before they turned fifteen, it was their mother's way of instilling in the young girls a sense of independence, for the time when it became necessary for them to move to their husband's home. Falmata was happy Ma'a had come to her pallet the night before. It had been a special privilege, and the little girl had felt really grateful. Her mother's presence had helped allay, just momentarily, the fear that was permanently lodged in Falmata's stomach, despite her many attempts to conquer it.

The driver swerved to avoid a particularly bad pothole. Falmata's stomach lurched.

'In the name of Allah the beneficial, the merciful,' she whispered the Suratul Fatiha, the very first words every Moslem says when praying, her fingers closing around and clicking each stone of the prayer beads her mother had given her as a going away gift. As her finger caressed each bead, she strove to concentrate on Allah as Ma'a had advised. But she couldn't.

Why did it have to be so hot today? Falmata stole a fleeting glance at the man traveling by her side.

The Silent One.

It wasn't his name, Falmata knew, she'd just decided in her mind to call him that. Other than the 'ruwa' he'd mumbled during their journey when she started coughing, followed by the handing over of a plastic bottle filled with warm, tepid water, he'd said nothing the entire journey. He hadn't even smiled when she thanked him for the water.

The goats mewed mournfully, again. Spying the bottle of water, one of them rose unsteadily from the floor of the truck and lumbered towards Falmata and her two companions.

The truck buckled as it hit a deep pothole. The young goat toppled across one of Malam Zarami's outstretched feet. The man shooed the animal away roughly. Then, as the driver regained control of the vehicle, the animal rose back up and tottered towards Falmata, and the plastic bottle in her hand. It stretched out a hot, dry tongue and began to lick at her hand.

Falmata tipped a little water into her palm and extended it to the thirsty animal. The first goat was quickly joined by the second one, and uttered a long 'miaaaah' of gratitude. They began to lick faster.

Falmata wiggled, moving her palm forward to make it more accessible to the gritty but comforting tongues of the animals at her feet.

'Be still!' Malam Zarami snapped, shooting her a long, disgruntled stare.

'Eh,' Falmata answered, and hurriedly withdrew her hand. The goats continued to nudge, their heads burrowing into her lap as they searched for her wet palm under the plastic bag containing her white abaya.

She hadn't wanted to wear her new, flowing white covering at home. Their village was located in a remote part of Borno State. The journey to Maiduguri, where the Khari market was situated, was going to be long, and dusty. She hadn't wanted to get her abaya dirty, or stained.

She wondered what everyone was doing back home at that moment. Ma'a had taken the goats out for their morning grass, right after the family had had their breakfast of kunu – the milk and sorghum porridge they ate every morning. Ba'a had protested that it was not her job.

'Let Kabir take them today,' he'd ordered, referring to her eight-year-old brother.

'I'll do it, Baranimin,' her mother had responded, pulling her abaya tightly around her as she did so. Falmata had sensed that her mother did not want to see her climb into the truck that was to take her away from this life.

Still, it was rare to see Ma'a disobey her father – especially in front of Alhaji Gambo, her father's eldest brother. Falmata had been fearful, as she waited for her father's response. Her father had not argued at her mother's decision, even though his brother's brow had darkened in annoyance. But he'd insisted she took Kabir with her. Ma'a's eyes were red and raw. Ma'a puffy eyes had become very common since Ba'a and his brothers' announcement of Falmata's special day.

Falmata knew the journey was making Ma'a sad. She'd wanted so much to hug and comfort her mother, but Alhaji Gambo had been watching intently. He did not approve of such open displays of emotion. For that reason, Falmata had taken to crawling into her mother's pallet on the nights her father wasn't there and wrapping her arms around her. It was an unusual experience; in their culture older girls did not seek such emotional contact with their mother. At first, her mother had lain stiff in Falmata's arms, but had soon submitted to her embrace. In the last days before her journey, the two had taken to entwining themselves so tightly it was hard to know where Falmata's body began and where her mother's ended. Falmata could sense the sadness wrapping itself around her mother like a thick blanket as the special day approached.

'You ought to be celebrating,' Uncle Gambo chastised her mother constantly; 'your own child – and a girl at that – chosen to perform such an honour. Not everyone is worthy of such privilege.'

'I am honoured, Alhaji. Allah be praised,' Ma'a had answered before lowering her eyes and pulling the upper part of her abaya tightly around her face.

So Falmata had said goodbye to her mother from a distance, before climbing into the truck.

Honour and privilege, the two words were her uncle's favourites. Falmata often wondered why Alhaji Gambo had not chosen one of his own daughters to go on this important and privileged journey. He had four girls, after all, and two of them were exactly Falmata's age. Why bestow their family with such honour? Everyone knew he did not like Falmata's mother or any of her children. The thought had baffled Falmata and she had posed the question to her mother once while they were preparing supper. 'Sssshhhh,' Ma'a had said, looking behind her shoulder, quickly covering Falmata's mouth with her palm. They were in the shack they used as a kitchen. The lower half of Falmata's face had been covered in white from the millet her mother had been grinding for the evening meal.

Everyone was afraid of her uncle, even Alhaji Yusuf, the Imam of their local Mosque. It wasn't just his stern and unsmiling bearded countenance. It was also his many friends who were, like him, bearded and unsmiling. She had heard her father whisper once that his brother had a connection to 'powerful Islamic groups.' Falmata knew that it would never have occurred to her father, or any of his brothers, to disagree with her uncle, Alhaji Gambo.

Besides being the oldest, Alhaji Gambo was the sole wealthy brother in the Kachalla family's household, the only one with a cement-walled and zinc-roofed house, instead of the mud huts scattered around the compound. Alhaji was also the only one of the four Kachalla brothers who had been able to afford the Hajj pilgrimage to Mecca. It was for that reason that the title, Alhaji, had been added to his name. Because of his financial status, Alhaji Gambo had paid the bridal price for Ba'a's second wife, Falmata's mother, and that of his third wife too. It was said that some had been surprised when Alhaji Gambo offered to pay Ba'a's bride price for Ma'a. Alhaji had been the first among the Kachalla boys to express interest in Zhara Abubakar, but her father had only agreed to give his daughter's hand to a Kachalla boy as long as that boy was not Gambo.

Some said Falmata's uncle never forgave the slight or forgot it.

Alhaji Gambo was the most devout Moslem in the village. But it was whispered that his devotion often bordered on the fanatic; although no one had ever dared to say that within his hearing – or the hearing of one of his ardent supporters. Malam Zarami was one of those supporters: He was Alhaji's closest cohort, and he was also the man to whom Zainab, Falmata's thirteen-year-old sister, was betrothed.

Falmata glanced from under her veil at Zainab's groom-to-be and shivered at the fate awaiting her gentle, graceful sister. She could not imagine living with such a stony-faced man.

Weddings were fun. Despite the man her sister was promised to, Falmata wished she could be around to witness Zainab's Fatiha. The Nanle gathering, where the bride's hand and feet were painted and decorated with henna, was always her favourite time during wedding ceremonies. It was the only day that girls in her community felt special, loved and pampered. For that reason, every young girl in their village longed for the day of their wedding ceremony: herself included.

Falmata wondered what it would be like where she was going. She had been told repeatedly that if you followed the five pillars of Islam, obeyed your Imam and all authority figures, you would not get to suffer in heaven as you do on earth. Also in heaven, Ma'a had told her that men and women were equal before Allah, with no one treating anyone else badly or wickedly.

'In heaven, we are all simply Allah's children, and, Al ham du Lilah, he does not tolerate one maltreating another.' There had been softness in her mother's voice and a longing in her eyes when she said that.

Despite the fear that gnawed at her intestines every now and then, Falmata was looking forward to being in such a place. Perhaps, in heaven, there would be no one as mean and as wicked as her uncle, Alhaji Gambo? Maybe she would even be allowed to play with other girls her age without being shouted at and told she was 'worthless and useless'?

Did people get married there? Falmata wondered also. If so, she hoped Allah would pick a good, and kind husband for her. Like Ali, she thought, thinking of the smiling face of her stepbrother's friend. Ali was fifteen, just five years older than her. She'd caught him stealing glances at her when he thought no one was looking, on the occasions that Falmata had been ordered to serve tea to her father and brother's visitors. Falmata herself had pretended to re-adjust her veil on those instances and let slip her head covering, revealing her face just briefly.

Falmata wiggled again in her seat, despite her fear of her sister's betrothed. The heat and the pain in her lower abdomen were making her lightheaded.

For her upcoming special event, Falmata had longed to wear a flowing white abaya – not the everyday dark one she wore when she took the goats out in search of grass. It was the most important event in her life, after all. Everyone knew white denotes purity. But, Falmata knew Ba'a was spending a lot of money on Zainab's upcoming nuptials, so she had not dared approach him with her request, even though he and their entire household had taken to treating her with uncharacteristic kindness as her special event drew near. Ma'a had promised to speak to Ba'a, but Falmata knew she was no less in awe of her father than Falmata herself was.

Ten days before the event, when the white abaya still wasn't forthcoming, Falmata realized her mother had not succeeded in convincing her father of the need to buy her the flowing white covering she coveted.

Falmata had turned to Hajiha Kolo.

Where the women were concerned, everyone knew her father's first wife was the power within Abdulkadir Kachalla's home. A full-born Kanuri woman, with the stubborn streak for which the people of this dry, rocky-terrain were renowned, she guarded that power jealously. Hajiha Aisha, Ba'a's third wife, a Fulani, had tried to contest the position when she was first brought in, but her father's first wife was not a woman one trifled with easily. The power she had managed to wrest for herself in the Kachalla home was hard won and she was not about to hand it over to some 'whey-faced Fulata Jiri,' no matter how pleasing her husband found the young and supple fair skin of his new wife.

In addition to ensuring that the big water gourds in Hajiha Kolo's section of the house were always full, Falmata took to caring for her stepmother's goats as well as their own.

Four days into her self-imposed extra-chores, Hajiha Kolo had handed her a plastic covered package.

'What is it, Hajiha? What should I do with it?' Falmata had enquired. Her stepmother had tweaked her cheek gently.

'Your white abaya, Yaa'na,' the older woman answered – having taken also to calling the young girl by that special term of endearment. 'All the extra work... do you think I was born yesterday?' Her stepmother chided kindheartedly.

The truck plunged into another pothole, jerking the occupants against one another.

Arching her left shoulder, Falmata attempted to dislodge a big, fat droplet of sweat she could feel snaking its way down the centre of her back.

Malam Zarami shot her another scornful look. She squirmed in discomfort.

They arrived at their destination in the early afternoon.

'Stand up! Get ready!' Malam Zarami barked, as the vehicle came to a stop some distance from the market. With a practiced flick of her hand, Falmata pulled off her everyday abaya and stood quietly as her sister's betrothed slipped the dark padded jacket over her head. He pulled the flaps at the sides, making the jacket tight and snug around her thin frame. The jacket was heavy and scratchy and some of the wires bit into her bare skin. Falmata winced. Again, her insides crawled with fear. In response to a curt nod from Malam Zarami, she unfurled the plastic bag she had brought with her. Taking out the white abaya, she passed it to her future uncle-to-be.

The man slipped the shiny, new abaya over her head; then he arranged the folds to camouflage the dark vest before tucking it securely in place. He moved aside the army-style blanket covering the opening of the back of the vehicle, then carefully deposited Falmata onto the dusty road.

'Remember, do nothing until you're exactly at the spot Malam Ali will indicate to you. Then follow the instructions I gave you. Do you remember... what to do?' he asked, pointing to a red button on the phone he had slipped into the right-hand pocket of her new abaya.

Falmata nodded, adding, 'Eh.'

'Go on then. Stay close to Malam Ali,' Malam Zarami said, signaling to the Silent One. 'Allah is great,' he added, before nudging her away from the descending ramp on the back of the dust-covered truck.

So that was his name... Malam Ali. He doesn't look like an Ali, Falmata thought, throwing a sidelong glance at her mute companion and comparing him to her fifteen-year-old stepbrother's friend. That one was always smiling, not like the ghostlike individual by her side.

The cramps were now a thousand tongues of needles in her stomach. Falmata glanced longingly at the bushes bordering both sides of the road; she wanted badly to wee-wee but didn't dare utter her request to either of her taciturn companions. So she started, again, to caress the prayer beads, which she had now transferred to the left pocket of her abaya.

'In the name of Allah the beneficial, the merciful...' her fingers sought comfort from the round smooth stones as she mouthed the well-remembered verse of the Suratul Fatiyah.

Just then a group of laughing young girls carrying their own calabash of Fura da nono passed by, jostling her as they did so. The edge of Falmata's white abaya swiped the dirty truck. Forgetting Malam's instructions for a moment, Falmata picked up her hem and began to shake the dust off vigorously.

'No sudden movements!' Malam Zarami barked angrily. Grabbing Falmata by her left ear, he pulled her back roughly towards the truck. Then he looked around furtively at the hordes of people hurrying back and forth on the busy road. No one was paying them any attention.

'Walahi! Are you deaf? I keep telling you. No sudden movements!'

Falmata nodded, her eyes watering from the pain in her throbbing ear.

Five hundred meters away, the noise from the teeming market could be heard clearly.

'Now go!' Malam Zarami ordered, nudging her forward once again.

'Eh,' she answered, turning around, walking towards the noise. The Silent One followed quietly beside her.

Halfway towards the centre of the market, The Silent One stopped. Pointing to an electric pole with a splash of red paint down the side, he uttered his first words of the day.

'There! That pole, go there.'

As Falmata turned in the direction he had indicated, the Silent One stopped her again. Then he did a curious thing. Laying one

27

hand lightly on her arm, he tilted her head up with his other hand. 'May Allah bless and truly grant you eternity in heaven,' he whispered gently, staring into her eyes. Then he let go of her before she could respond. Finally, he too nudged her towards the marked electric pole and turned, walking hurriedly in the opposite direction.

Falmata watched his departing back until it disappeared into the market crowd. For a reason she could not fully understand, Falmata was deeply touched by the man's gesture. Still baffled, she turned once more in the direction he had instructed and steeled herself to complete her assignment.

Falmata had barely gone a few steps when she felt deep, piercing pain from her stomach, followed by a warm flow down one side of her leg. Momentarily confused, she looked down... and panicked.

It was the curse. Ma'a had warned her about it. Now she understood why she had been feeling so weak and dizzy throughout the trip. Her curse – Ma'a said it was the scourge of every woman and that it happened every month – had finally appeared when she least expected. Ma'a had also said that its appearance meant a girl had now reached womanhood... that she was now fully ready for marriage.

Falmata did not mind being a woman. Perhaps now Ali would tell his parents to approach Ba'a for her hand in marriage? She was now a woman... fully a woman.

Falmata looked down again. No, she did not mind being a woman. She just minded having her shiny, white abaya stained... which it now was.

She didn't want to continue with the journey in this condition.

No, not any longer... not like this, she shook her head dejectedly. Without calling it by name, her uncle had made it known to the females of his family that the curse was the dirtiest thing that could befall any woman. As far as Falmata had come to learn, a woman with the curse was neither worthy to be seen by any man nor was she worthy to prepare any meal that was to be eaten by a man, because such a woman was dirty, not pure. Falmata had wanted to be pure when she stood in front of Allah. For that reason, she'd taken particular care with her toiletry that morning. In addition to cleaning her fingernails and toenails with a needle-like twig she'd picked off the ground in the women's bath area, she had also paid special care to the dirty cracks on the back of her feet. Using the pumice stone from Ma'a's plastic soap dish, she'd scrubbed her feet until the dirt was completely sloughed from the soles.

And now, she was all stained and dirty – unworthy to stand before Allah. And if she was unworthy and dirty, how then could she enjoy all the good in heaven she had heard so much about? Surely, Allah would not permit a dirty, stinky female all covered in the curse to stand in his revered presence?

No. She couldn't do it! Since she could not have heaven she wanted to go home. To be married, perhaps one day to Ali? She wasn't sure if marrying Ali would make life more bearable than in their home, but it didn't matter so much. Whenever her uncle Alhaji Gambo demanded obedience that was particularly difficult, her Ma'aa always told her, 'Yaa,na the suffering on earth is temporary, do what he says.' But she wasn't going to have heaven now with the curse all over her, was she? Falmata thought.

She stood in the middle of the teeming crowd and turned in the direction she and Silent One had come a few minutes earlier. She scanned the jam-packed crowd for his familiar face. She needed to tell him she'd changed her mind... that she wanted to go home: she was stained, she was impure. But she was a woman now. Ali... imagine having Ali for a husband? His smiling...

She didn't hear the explosion, as her body blew apart before the deafening blast even reached her ears. She hadn't clicked the red button, as Malam Zarami had instructed. Amidst the mayhem, the blood, the screaming, the panic, two figures silently skulked back towards a waiting vehicle. One of them fingered a remote device in his pocket. He knew better by now than to trust such a youngster. The other is as silent as ever, but prays to Allah to have mercy on the child's soul.

NANA ends the story with the traditional 'Ekong-nke-e,'

Instead of responding in the traditional way, Esit-Ima says, 'Oh, that girl! That poor, poor little girl.' Her voice is shaky.

Nana lowers her head and mutters, almost inaudibly, 'Indeed, the poor, poor girl.'

'And the mother, the poor, sad mother,' Esit-Ima, continues. The old woman's head jerks up as if she had been waiting to hear Esit-Ima say that.

'Did you just say, the poor, sad mother? Weren't you ready to have her tarred and feathered at the beginning of the tale?'

'Yes, Nana, but I didn't know the full story then. I had no idea!'

'Ehn, ehn. See, now you have come to the lesson I wanted you to learn from this story. And that lesson is this: never be quick to judge and condemn until you possess the full knowledge, the absolute full knowledge, of the situation you are judging, and condemning. You see, dear child, there are layers to everything that happens in this world; layers to every issue argued and presented. Layers that the one who is not directly connected to it can ever truly understand.'

'Yes, Nana, I...'

'Shsssh, do not interrupt, Koko-Ima. This is the time for you to listen, not to speak.' The old woman picks up the jug of juice and takes another mouthful. She continues. 'Unless you are directly linked to an event, and have a full understanding of its whys and wherefores, do not jump to judge, my child. Do not jump to condemn.'

The grandmother stops suddenly, cups her left ear with one veined hand. Pom-pom-pom, the sound of a mortar being pounded echoes from the courtyard beyond.

'We will continue with this later. I believe I hear your mother making preparations for supper. She will have need of your help. Besides, I believe the news of the hour is about to come through.' Just as she predicts, the radio warbles, followed by a short fanfare of music. *'This is the six o'clock news…'*

That night, Esit-Ima cannot sleep. She turns and tosses, thinking of Falmata. She had heard stories of the suicide bombings happening up North. But until Falmata's story, she'd never given a human face to the suicide bombers themselves. In her mind, they had always been 'those terrible, evil people.' Nothing had resonated until last night. Now she begins to wonder. What were the stories behind the suicide bombers? The men, the women and children who caused such untold suffering? Who were the families? What kind of dynamics made up their surroundings? What challenges did they face daily? Did they have someone to turn to, someone with whom to share their fears, their sorrows, their secrets? Did they have someone who loved them as her Nana loved her? What of the really young children? What kind of future did they dream about? Esit-Ima was brought up to view God as love. What was their understanding of God? All the things she takes for granted, like hugging her mother, the freedom to express her opinions and her ability to complain loudly when she was dissatisfied with the minutest aspect of her life — How horrible to know that another child, another young person, did not have that kind of freedom or opportunity.

The following morning dawns bright and beautiful. Bird calls wake up the community, along with the swish, swish sound of brooms on bare ground as the villagers clean their compound and prepare for another day, heralding a new life, a life filled with hope, the hope that Falmata never had. Esit-Ima could not feel the joy she used to feel at the morning sounds all around her. Her heart lays heavy and unresponsive in her chest.

'What is the matter, Koko-nmi?' her Nana asks as Esit-Ima brought the old woman's breakfast of corn pap and fried bean cake.

'Nothing, Nana!' Esit-Ima says, putting down the tray at the efe. Her Nana prefers to eat her meals there when she wants time alone with her beloved radio.

'Nothing? Then why are your eyes covered with sackcloth?'

Esit-Ima smiles at her Nana's usual reference to sadness. She does not want the old woman to worry, so she says again, 'Nothing.'

The old woman takes her face between two bony palms and looks deep into her eyes. Esit-Ima lowers her eyes.

'You forget I know you well, my heart. If I had passed before you were born, one would have said you were my spirit come back to the family, you do know that, don't you?'

Esit-Ima nods.

'Then why do you lie to an old woman who is the other side of your soul? Tell me what the matter is.'

'I keep thinking of Falmata, of the story you told yesterday.'

'It makes you sad for her, does it?'

Esit-Ima nods. 'Yes.'

'Then sit here, let me tell you another story; one that will erase The White Abaya from your eyes... at least for the moment.'

'But, Nana, there's no time. Mother wants me to go for the fitting of my traditional outfit at Mama Sisi's shop.'

33

'There is always time for a story, my heart. Besides, this one is short. It is called 'Madam Shopkeeper.' It will not take long to tell.'

'Should I go and get the others to join us?'

'No. Not this time, my heart. This story is yours and yours alone. Come! Sit! *Ekong nke-e.*'

'*Nke ekong Abasi. Ekong aka, ekong oyong, ekong isi maha udim.*'

Madam Shopkeeper

(First published in *Payback and Other Stories:
An Anthology of African and African Diaspora Short Stories*)

BIBIANA got off the motorcycle, paid the biker, hefted up her traveling bag with her right hand and walked into her father's compound. It was 6.45pm, almost dinner time, and she could hear its preparation over the courtyard behind the house. The drive from Lagos had taken more than twelve hours and she was bone-tired. Nonetheless, she dragged her feet as she walked along the side of the house toward the yard.

Her family didn't know she was coming home.

The first person to see Bibiana was Kubiat, her fourteen-year-old stepsister.

'Mama! Mama! Bibiana is back!' the girl yelled into an opened doorway where a whirl of bulbous smoke was issuing from a fireplace.

Kubiat had been grinding something in the mortar. The pom-pom sound Bibiana had heard came from her. She now stopped and regarded Bibiana with a blank expression. In the far corner of the veranda, Ediye, Kubiat's seventeen-year-old sister was having her hair braided by a woman Bibiana recognized as their neigbour's second wife. Bibiana greeted both women. While the woman moved over to Bibiana to hug her,

35

Ediye simply looked at Bibiana. 'You are back,' she said without much warmth.

'I am back,' Bibiana responded equally briskly and then turned back to Kubiat.

'Goodness, how you've grown! You were so little when I left and now look at you... almost as tall as me!' Bibiana dropped her traveling bag, moved towards the young girl and squeeze-hugged her. The younger girl continued to gape, making no move to return Bibiana's embrace.

A moment later a light-complexioned woman emerged from the kitchen.

She was heavyset and round. Rolls of flesh escaped from the sleeveless flowered dress she was wearing, bulging from underneath her armpits.

'Good evening Mma,' Bibiana moved forward and bowed to her stepmother.

'What're you doing here?' Koko-Eka's eyes raked her from head to toe and then back again.

Before Bibiana could respond the rest of her family appeared.

Bibiana was especially happy to see Joy, her sister, who was twenty-two. Even when she was still a child herself, Joy had played the role of a mother when their mother passed away. Bibiana had been nine years old and Joy barely eleven.

They all wanted to know why she hadn't told them she was coming home.

'Bibiana will tell us in her own good time. Let her have a drink of water and wash the dust from the trip off her body first,' Bibiana's father said.

Bibiana told them as they were having dinner.

'Is that it?' her father's voice was tinged with puzzlement. 'We've always known this to be your dream.'

Bibiana exchanged a look with Joy. Was her father just naïve or deliberately obtuse? She looked over at her stepmother; the woman continued to section off the fufu and then dipped it in the soup – eating as if completely unaware of the conversation.

Bibiana had always known she was born to be a schoolteacher. From the moment she could join the alphabet together to spell out her name, it was her most ardent dream. 'Let's do everything in our power to make it come true,' her mother used to say to her father. 'As soon as she passes her O'levels, she'll go to the Teachers' Training College in Edem,' Bibiana's father affirmed.

But before she was ten, a series of events conspired to derail her ambition. First, her father married a second wife. Then her mother died giving birth, a stillbirth; and finally, right after her O'level exams, Bibiana was carted off to Lagos to become the house servant to the owner of a Buka, a local eatery in the centre of the city. Her stepmother had arranged it.

Bibiana's stepmother, Koko-Eka, was an entrepreneur. From salt to flip-flops, bread and crayfish to soap, if it could be sold, battered, and brokered, Koko-Eka could do it. That was why everyone in Ibom called her Madam Shopkeeper.

But everyone in Ibom village knew her to be mean-spirited. Greedy too. Despite being one of the wealthiest people in a place where day-to-day living was hard; despite being one of the very few who could afford to feed her family rice at Christmas, Bibiana's stepmother was never satisfied with what she had. Nor did she hesitate to manipulate others, friends and foes alike, into giving up the little they had.

'She has the integrity of a tropical mosquito! More than two years of doing business together and she treats me that way?' A visiting palm-oil buyer who'd just been tricked by Koko-Eka into buying a van-load of fresh oil mixed with rancid leftover oil complained.

Koko-Eka's meanness was not reserved for strangers alone. She did not treat Bibiana's father well. He was an unassuming gentleman with a permanently stooped posture. Bibiana knew many in their village referred to him behind his back as Madam Shopkeeper's Handbag.

'Yap! Yap! Yap! Morning and night! I am tired of her voice in this house. Why's she not letting any water your father drinks stay in his stomach? Her own mother is exactly like her. Bad fruit from bad tree...tfffiaqua!' Bibiana's mother used to complain.

What propelled a gentle soul like Joshua Imoh into marrying a woman like Koko-Eka? One day Bibiana overheard a group of villagers discussing her family.

'Couldn't resist her ample, seductive backside,' someone amongst them said.

'Long throat,' another scorned. Even in her teens, Koko-Eka was not poor. 'That woman has been an ardent trader for a long time.' Before she was barely out of her diapers, her own mother used to boast.

As to why Koko-Eka married Joshua Imoh? Bibiana's mother used to offer a different explanation.

'She wanted a title. Mrs. Headmaster was making the foolish girl's head swell, so she had to rush in here to snatch the crown she was convinced I wore.'

Perhaps her mother was right, Bibiana thought. Unfortunately for her stepmother, Bibiana's father's title did not come with many tangible benefits. And three children later—two girls and a boy—the only beings she showered with love, Koko-Eka could still be heard tongue-lashing Bibiana's father in public and lamenting his inability to play the role of a man. It did not help matters that Joshua Imoh's job brought little cash into the household, making Koko-Eka the official breadwinner in her husband's home. Despite her stepmother's unreasonable behaviour, never once did Bibiana's father defend himself or his children. That made it easy for her to see why many said her father had ceded the proverbial trousers to the truculent Koko-Eka the moment she entered their home as a young, but even then, not at all gentle or accommodating bride.

Bibiana was16 years old when she left for Lagos. The woman she was sent to serve was an old friend of Koko-Eka from their primary school days. Her stepmother had arranged everything. She also insisted that Bibiana's pay was sent home.

'Your father will keep it for you until you're ready to take up your studies. Otherwise, you'll end up spending the lot. I know you young girls. Reach Lagos now and you'll want to buy every latest, shiny, useless thing you see.'

Bibiana's sojourn in Lagos and her service to Madam Buka was to be temporary, just long enough to help her save up the start-up fees for her teacher's training college.

'You know the situation with my job,' her father had said. 'As we speak, the government has not paid my salary or that of the teachers under me for more than six months. You won't be there for longer than a year.' Her father had promised.

Bibiana had ended up staying in Lagos for four years. Her stepmother was responsible for the prolonged stay.

'You need to earn a bit more money; your father's job is just face-service. It no longer brings in any money. My own business isn't going as well as it used to.'

The excuses were endless and varied. Bibiana knew her dream would remain exactly that, a dream unless she took matters into her own hands. Then she received a letter from her sister.

'Koko-Eka is keeping your salary, not Papa,' Joy wrote.

Bibiana had suspected as much. Joy also told her of Koko-Eka's reaction when their father had gently suggested that Bibiana's money ought, perhaps, to be in Joy's safekeeping.

'This is not your idea, Joshua, I know it. Joy has put you up to this, admit it. What does she think I'll do with her sister's miserable money? Swallow it? Has she forgotten what I am called in this town? Madam Shopkeeper. That's right! That name didn't just get handed over to me for nothing. It's because I get money... proper money... not just some nonsense kobo, kobo!'

'I had to stay completely out of her way for more than a week. She was that livid! Please don't let on that you know,' Joy wrote.

Bibiana kept her promise, which was why she first approached her father the morning following her arrival.

'Your stepmother has it. It's in her account, kept safe for you,' her father replied.

Bibiana went to her stepmother.

'What money?' Koko-Eka's voice was a study in nonchalance.

'My pay... 4,500 Naira... multiplied by four years. That would be...'

'Please let me not hear another word!' Koko-Eka lashed out. 'Who got the nonsense job for you in the first place? Also, all the years I fed you; all the years I toiled; taking care of your sister who won't marry and live in her husband's home like other girls her age. You think I vomited the money I used in doing that? Or plucked it from a tree?'

Bibiana's mouth hung open.

'But Mma, she's Papa's child too, this is her home...'

'Wai-wai-wai! Is this what they taught you in Lagos? This rudeness to your seniors; to your elders?' Koko-Eka heaved her copious weight off the stool on which she was perched. 'Papa's child, too,' she mimicked. 'So she's Papa's child, too, is she? Ask your useless father. How much does he contribute to the upkeep in this house? Tell me that, Miss She's-Papa's-Child-Too. All these years... I looked after you all as if you were mine... toiled like a Hebrew slave to an Egyptian king, I did; worked my fingers to the bone,' Koko-Eka waved her pudgy hand dramatically in Bibiana's face.

Bibiana was dismayed, but her stepmother was just getting started. Sweat broke out all over Koko-Eka as she ranted. She stomped up and down the wrapper she had tied sarong-like across her bulging bosom bunched up behind her wobbly backside, the folds creasing between the crack.

Bibiana begged and pleaded but to no avail. Koko-Eka refused to part with Bibiana's savings. Bibiana turned to her father. But the cowed, stooped figure proved to be of little help.

Nine months following her return home, Bibiana could still not find a solution to her dilemma.

And then a suitor came calling.

Moses was the son of the first wife of a Chief in the neighbouring village. His father was famed for his many farmlands and his cocoa farms. Marriage wasn't part of Bibiana's immediate plans but it was rumoured that Chief Solo was planning to open shops for his three wives, including Moses's mother, in Ibeto, a teeming transit town of about 100,000 inhabitants.

It was still a rumour, but surely, a man whose father was that wealthy could afford to send his own wife to school, Bibiana thought. Besides, and most importantly, Moses himself, a man of twenty-five, had just completed his first degree in Business Administration. In a region where having a university degree was akin to visiting the moon that was a big deal, indeed. 'A young man like that wasn't going to settle for his wife being illiterate, was he?' she mused.

Bibiana turned her full attention to Moses's proposal. Should she be thinking of marriage so early in life?

'I thought she wanted to go to school' Koko-Eka complained when Moses's family approached her father to formally state its intentions.

If there was another thing Bibiana's stepmother was known for, it was her reluctance to let others shine. Forget the age-old adage that competition is good for business. If Koko-Eka had her way, none but she would own a shop in their entire Local Government area. Marrying into a family that could one day, possibly, compete with her for the title of Madam Shopkeeper was a thought that drenched Koko-Eka's armpit in cold sweat, and Bibiana knew it. She could feel the animosity oozing from her stepmother's pores.

'Here!' Koko-Eka said, four days before Moses's family was to visit, thrusting a brown envelope at Bibiana.

'What is it, Mma?' Bibiana enquired, the envelope held loosely in one hand. The rest of the family looked on, baffled.

'Just open it! Her stepmother commanded. 'You children of nowadays. Always asking unnecessary questions.'

Bibiana tore open the brown envelope.

Wads of dirty Naira notes tumbled out.

She looked up, uncomprehending; then turned to her father. Joshua Imoh's face mirrored that of his daughter's.

'After thinking long and hard, I've managed to run up and down to gather the money you need for your teacher's training. Education's very important, you know? Girls these days… they must be educated; otherwise, their husbands make doormats of them,' Koko-Eka's voice was laden with self-righteous importance.

In all the years since becoming a member of the Imoh's household, Koko-Eka's vampiric ways had prevented Bibiana and her sister from forming any affection for her. Now, seventeen years of mutual animosity completely forgotten, Bibiana rushed forward to embrace her stepmother, gratitude spilling out of her voice as she thanked Koko-Eka over and over again.

It did occur to her to wonder at her stepmother's sudden, inexplicable generosity; after all, Koko-Eka was not known to perform any act of kindness that did not directly benefit her. But the thought did not stay in her head for long; her dream was finally coming true. She wasn't about to look a gift goat in the mouth.

Six weeks later she hopped on the motorcycle her father had hired and made the 35km ride trip to the Higher Learning

Teacher's Training College in Edem. What had changed Koko-Eka's mind months into Bibiana's program? Everything was made clear. It came in another brown envelope, this time from Joy.

Bibiana ripped the envelope open, wondering what was so important that it couldn't wait until the end of her first term, which was in less than ten days.

'Ediye and Moses are engaged. Chief Solo's family is coming next week Saturday to ask Papa for Ediye's hand officially,' the letter read.

Ediye was Koko-Eka's oldest daughter.

Bibiana blinked. She had wondered why Moses was no longer visiting and why his letters had stopped coming within six weeks of her being in school. The excitement of getting the education she'd always wanted had prevented her from dwelling on the subject. Everything began to make sense. Koko-Eka's unusual kindness; her influence in making sure the school accepted Bibiana even though it was already one week into its semester… When would her stepmother ever stop? Bibiana wondered again for the umpteenth time what could have possessed her father to marry such a woman. She perused the content of the letter once again.

The thought of returning to her father's household was not pleasant. But where else could she go?

The three week holiday was awful. Bibiana and her stepsiblings were never close at the best of times; now, whipped up by their mother, they did everything they could to make her life and Joy's unbearable. She felt sorry for her sister, but Bibiana could not wait to get back to school.

A few months later, a young man of about thirty bought a piece of land connecting their village to the next and started to create a huge open-plan building and a smaller one off to one side. No one knew who the man was or where he had come from.

'But it's obvious he's very, very rich. You should see the jeep he drives... a real tear-tire, I tell you!' Joy wrote.

Bibiana read the letter and could not help laughing at her big sister's description of the stranger's ultra-modern SUV.

'What more do you know about him other than the fact that he drives a 'tear-tire?' Bibiana wrote back.

'Koko-Eka made some discoveries. Turns out he lives in America and he's unmarried. Here's the biggest irony... Koko-Eka is now wishing she hadn't pushed Ediye on Moses. I know she wishes Ediye was free. This new guy is much richer than Moses!' her sister replied in her next letter.

Bibiana's lip tightened at the last piece of news. And then she exploded with laughter. But the sound was anything but mirthful. Back in her village, the building continued and Joy kept her sister up-to-date with its progress.

'The scaffolding has gone up all around the stranger's structure,' Joy wrote two weeks before Bibiana was to return home again on holiday. 'No one has ever seen anything quite like it. No one has ever before been so secretive about putting up a building. It's more beautiful than anything we've ever seen, but he won't say a thing about it. It's a complete mystery.'

'What can it mean?' Bibiana wrote back.

Two weeks later she arrived home in time for the formal opening of the stranger's structure. Everyone in Ibom village was invited. A special invitation was sent to the Chief. Bibiana had hardly dropped her bag when her sister propelled her towards the music and merriment.

It was a lavish celebration. The stranger had brought in caterers: rice and stew, pounded yam and Edikan-ikong soup, Afia-efere. These was so much food and drink... the celebration was only an hour underway and already the speech of some of the men – young and old alike – were slurred.

'Look at all this,' Joy declared with a sweeping gesture of one hand. 'I told you he was rich,' she turned to Bibiana. 'He's really handsome, too' she added, a wistful note in her voice.

'You've fallen in love, I see,' Bibiana joked.

'Not hard to. Just wait until you see him,' her sister promised.

Minutes later Christopher Samson – for that was the stranger's name – emerged. He was wearing a pair of jeans and a white embroidered shirt and brown-patterned shoes. The outfit was completed with a wide, brown-snake-skin belt. The outfit complemented a tall, lean physique, a head of dark baby-like curls and a broad face cupped by a warm smile.

'You were not lying,' Bibiana whistled under her breath.

An old woman standing nearby heard Bibiana's comment and turned with a toothless grin to the two sisters.

'The most beautiful man I've ever seen. What I wouldn't give to be young again with a full set of teeth.' She was the town's octogenarian, a woman renowned for her self-deprecating wit. The two girls giggled.

When everyone had gathered and the party was in full swing, Christopher asked the DJ to lower the volume on the sound system. Then he began to speak.

First, he bowed towards the Chief and members of his council; then he thanked everyone else for coming, telling them it was a privilege to become a member of their community and promised to contribute to its development.

'And now, it gives me great honour to announce the opening of...' At this, he stopped and gestured to a group of five men standing on either side of the shrouded structures.

They pulled down the billowing grey plastic. The first structure on the side was revealed: a bungalow painted in yellow, army-green and grey trimmings.

Everyone gasped! It was the most beautiful building everyone there had ever seen, Bibiana included.

'How can anyone build something like that in less than one year?' Bibiana heard someone whisper.

'Na money, my brother. Sweet, sweet money,' another added. 'See, see, see...' he continued, seemingly loss for words.

'I agree with you, my brother. Only real money can cook okra soup, I swear; nothing but the best ingredients can turn a boring vegetable like okra into a dish fit for a king,' yet another said.

As most were still gawking at the beautiful bungalow, the team of five men threw off the plastic on the bigger structure. If the first edifice was worthy of a gasp, the second one took their breath away. It was a shop: the biggest everyone gathered there had ever seen. And it wasn't empty. As if controlled by an invisible button, the villagers, all without exception, moved forward, stopped, and peered. The cavernous structure was stocked from top to bottom with goods of every description: rows of glittering cans, umbrellas, all kinds of soaps, cans of beverages, sugar – one whole section had stacks of bread and biscuits. There were different brands of beer, rows, and rows of wine and spirits... everything anyone could imagine. There was even a shelf loaded with flip-flops and rain boots.

The place was amazing enough, but what stopped everyone in their stride was the big neon sign... in purple and gold. Splayed across its glittering surface were the words, MADAM BIBIANA'S SHOP.

'Bibiana? Who's Bibiana' Joy turned to her sister with a puzzled expression.

Bibiana shrugged. 'I don't know. What're you staring at me for?' She shrugged again as her sister rotated her attention back to the shop.

Joy was not the only one whose focus was rotating back and forth between Bibiana and the shop. Bibiana's name was unusual. Other than their immediate family, no one else knew how her father had happened upon a name none in the community had ever heard until hers.

'Your father named you after a woman who saved his life long ago when he was twelve years old. She took your father to a hospital when a hit-and-run driver left him for dead on the side of a road,' Bibiana's mother had explained.

'She was my savior. Not only did she take me to the hospital, but she also paid for a bed,' her father had added.

As the assembly continued to ponder the name of the shop and their neighbour's daughter's unusual name, Christopher Samson turned and walked toward Bibiana. She, in turn, also walked towards him. As the villagers watched them come together, the man who had first arrived in their community a year previously reached out and dropped a set of keys into

Joshua Imoh's outstretched palm and gently closed her fingers over the jangling bunch.

'For you, my love. Happy 21st birthday.'

'Thank you, Chris. Come!' So saying, Bibiana walked, hand-in-hand, with Christopher to where members of her family were standing, open-mouthed, eyes disbelieving.

As she passed Joy, Bibiana bumped her elder sister playfully on the shoulder.

'If you don't close your mouth, sister, you'll swallow all the flies in this village,' she teased.

'Huh, huh' Joy muttered; her throat bobbed up and down in disbelief. Then her mouth snapped wide open again as her little sister pulled Christopher Samson over to their father and Koko-Eka and said:

'Papa, please meet Christopher, the man I'm going to marry.'

'Pleased to meet you, Sir,' Christopher reached forward, pulled the befuddled Joshua Imoh's hand out and pumped it respectfully up and down. The older man's mouth, like those of the rest of his family, remained wide open.

Next, Bibiana turned and walked back to her sister's side. Joy was still incapable of moving. Unable to contain the smile spreading across her face, Bibiana reached forward, took her older sister's hand and repeated a gesture similar to the one her fiancé had performed a few minutes before. She spread open the palm of Joy's right hand, dropped the keys Christopher had given her into her sister's hand and closed her fingers gently, lovingly over it.

'You'll have to live there,' she pointed at the bungalow, 'and run this,' her hand gestured towards the shop. 'Chris is taking me to America in six weeks. I will complete my studies there.'

49

'Huh, huh,' Joy muttered stupidly, again.

Bibiana laughed out loud, which seemed to break some kind of spell, as everyone began to speak at the same time.

'Congratulations, Sir!'

'Congratulations, Headmaster!'

As they crowded around the dazed Joshua Imoh, pumping his hand up and down, a big smile slowly broke across Bibiana's father's face and he stood straight, his shoulders no longer stooped.

And then the crowd turned towards Bibiana.

'Madam Shopkeeper! Congratulations!' they crowed.

Bibiana looked over to her stepmother. The woman and her children still stood motionless, an idiotic look on their faces. Then she turned towards the crowd, pointed one finger in the direction of her older sister and said, 'I am not Madam Shopkeeper. I wish to be Madam Teacher. Joy is Madam Shopkeeper now.'

NANA chants *'Ekong-nke-e,'* and Esit-Ima responds *'Nke ekong Abasi'* in a loud and happy voice.

'Oh, Nana, what a beautiful, beautiful story,' she says and gives the old woman a hug. Then she jumps up and dances around the efe. 'Good for Bibiana! Serves that wicked Koko-Eka woman right!' Nana looks at her and shakes her head back and forth in amusement. 'How you jump about, dear child; so unseemly for a young girl with a full bosom. You do know that you are now a young lady, no longer a child, don't you?' she reprimands.

But her voice is light and her eyes twinkle with amusement. She is pleased that her story has taken her Esit-Ima's focus off the troubling tale of the previous day. She is glad the young girl no longer has the sackcloth eyes with which she first came into the hut. Still, she wants to make sure it is not only joy at Koko-Eka's comeuppance that Esit-Ima is celebrating. So, she asks: 'What have you learned from the story, my heart?'

'Not to mistreat other people's children.'

'Yes, that's one point.' Nana lifts up her left hand and then bends the little finger on that hand with the right one in a counting symbol. 'And?'

'Not to be greedy, not to seek for one's happiness and success at the expense of others.'

'That's two and three,' the old woman presses down her ring and middle fingers simultaneously.

'The good we do comes back to us, so too does the bad we do.'

'Good. Go on.'

'Only God determines the future of every man. We should never treat others as though we hold their future in our hands.'

'Mmmmm, yes, yes. Next?' By now the old woman has stopped counting. Her hands lay folded in her lap, her eyes train on Esit-Ima, whose face is scrunching up in concentration as she enumerates the many the lessons she has learned from Madam Shopkeeper.

'Yes, well, Nana, the story just teaches one to behave with kindness and integrity at all times.'

'True. But how does it relate to you? How would you apply it to yourself?'

'Apply it to me? Nana, have you forgotten that I am still single? How can I apply the story of a woman with two step-daughter and several children of her own? Besides, Benjie would never ever look at another woman... he loves me too much... so the talk of stepchildren does not apply to me.'

'That's where you are wrong, my heart. The foundations of adult life are laid in infancy. If the foundations are not built with the essential lessons and values of life, then how can that life be anything but chaotic and in shambles? I wish you only the good and not the bad of life, Koko-Ima. But it would be improper of me to prepare you for only the good. And so, never plan your life based on what you think another can or cannot do. The road of life, my heart, can hand one who travels on it anything at any time.'

'I know Benjie, Nana.'

'Yes, I know you know him, Koko-nmi, but a wise person is one who trains his heart to deal rightly with all kinds of circumstances, even if those circumstances never happen.'

Esit-Ima thinks about her Nana's advice as she makes her way to her fitting.

It is while she is at the dressmaker's shop that she learns of the arrest of Inem Ibanga's husband. 'About time that happened,' another woman being fitted said. Esit-Ima could not wait to report news of the arrest to her Nana.

Inem Ibanga's tale is well known in their community and those around it. She has become the town's cautionary tale. It is a sad tale, as she is a battered wife. Her mother-in-law used to be Nana's closest friend until a year before when the two fell out because Nana had taken the case to the town's council of elders. She had demanded that Okon Ibanga was called to order for the constant abuse of his wife. Her Nana had always been outspoken, but many felt that she had gone too far this time. 'A man's trouble with his wife is a private matter, to be dealt with within the family unless that family chooses to call in an outsider. That is our custom,' they said.

Nana was furious with impotent rage.

After her fitting, Esit-Ima hurries home with the news.

'Oh, my heart is glad this day,' the old woman flattens one palm against her chest and taps it repeatedly. 'So glad. Did they say who called the police?'

This is the part Esit-Ima has been looking forward to sharing. 'Granny Ibanga,' she says simply.

'Aret Ibanga! Aret Ibanga called the police on her own son? Good for her! Good for that brave young woman!'

Esit-Ima burst out laughing. The woman her Nana had just called 'young woman' is nothing short of seventy. Her Nana is the oldest person in the village and as far as she's concerned anyone not as old as she is is young.

'They say Granny Ibanga has personally requested that the

police keep her son in jail for at least a month. The entire village is agog at the news, Nana. Nothing like this has ever happened before, they say. No parent has ever called the police on their own son or had him locked up. They say Grandpa Ibanga must be rolling in his grave at the 'shame' his wife's actions have brought on the family's name.'

'Shame! Shame. What happened to the 'shame' of a grown man beating his wife, the woman who gave birth to his children? Demeaning and disgracing her right in front of those very children's eyes? Human beings, I will never understand human beings,' the old woman shakes her head back and forth.

'But it is good that he has been arrested at last, isn't it? So, all is now well.' Just then, the radio emits a big gurgle and a voice comes through. '*The Senate President has...*'

Nana leans forward and lowers its volume. She turns to Esit-Ima. 'All is well? How can all be well as long as men like Okon Ibanga still roam this earth, kicking their wives around like footballs? Have you forgotten what Sunday Iton did to his wife last week?'

Nana was referring to another case of spousal abuse in their village in which a husband had taken off his wife's ear. When brought before their Chief and asked why he had done this terrible thing, he replied simply, 'She is a stubborn woman and does not listen to me. Perhaps now she will.'

Her Nana continues, 'Why do some men still think an act of violence towards their wife is proof of their virility and strength? Mark my word, payback eventually comes to such men. Unfortunately, when it happens, it affects both the good and the innocent around them. I have tried telling these men, I have tried telling the Council of Chiefs to reign in these men, but will they listen to me? No.

'Come,' Nana beckons to Esit-Ima even though the young girl is already sitting at her feet, 'I want to tell you another story, a story of what can happen when wrongs are not righted in a timely manner.'

'Esit-Ima! Eeessssit-Ima!' her name explodes somewhere beyond the courtyard of their home. 'Esit-Ima!' It is the voice of her mother, coming closer.

'Nana, I don't think I can hear another story now. There isn't time—'

'There's always time for a story, my heart.'

'But from the urgency in her voice, Mama needs me.' Her mother comes through the door of the main house as Esit-Ima finishes speaking. She watches as her mother crosses the short distance and enters the efe. She is not alone. Esit-Ima's father is with her.

'Good day, Ekamba-Mma,' both greet the old woman.

'Good day, son. Good day, beloved wife,' Nana smiles.

'Beloved wife' is the term of endearment she uses for all five wives of all her five sons. Esit-Ima's mother sometimes jokingly asks her, if we are all beloved, Ekamba-Mma, how can we tell which amongst us you love the most?' To which her Nana always responds, 'All of you. I love all of you the most.'

'Mama, I was just about to come to you and...' Esit-Ima begins.

'It's story-time,' Nana says simply.

Her parents exchange looks. 'Oh,' they say.

'It's okay, Nana, I will go and help Mother with...'

'Stay! Hear what your Nana has to say,' her father interrupts. Both her parents look at the old woman again and smile.

And Esit-Ima realizes something then. This new style in which her Nana delivers the stories to her and her alone, despite the many other young people in their compound, which comprises more than five buildings, is deliberate. Everyone knows the closeness between her and her Nana. They also know she is getting married and leaving the family home soon. This is their gift to her... allowing her more time with her beloved grandmother. Esit-Ima looks at her parents with gratitude. Then she turns to the old lady.

'Tell me the story then, Nana, please,' she implores as her parents turn to leave.

'*Ekong nke-e.*'

'*Nke ekong Abasi. Ekong aka, ekong oyong, ekong isi maha udim.*'

When The Cock Crows

ELIZABETH wiggled a little on the raffia mat, trying to work the kinks out of her bottom, as she waited to be summoned. She looked down her legs, and then her hands; both were bound with three-corded raffia rope. It was becoming harder to ignore the itching and cramps that came from sitting in one position for so long.

It won't be long now, she thought and moved her spine back and forth against the wall of the mud hut to relieve some of her discomfort. She scanned the dimly lit room, its form made distinguishable only by the rays of the sun slanting through the cracks along the wooden door, and the lone wooden window directly opposite where she was sitting. The place was bare, except for the mat, an unlit kerosene lamp, and a tray containing two plates: one holding a large ball of fufu and the other, some kind of vegetable soup.

The dish was untouched. She had no interest in food. Her children were safe. That was what counted. For that reason, she was determined to take her secret to the grave.

As for her fate, she thought, hers had been settled the moment she took the first swing of that axe. She accepted that.

Through the cracks in the door, Elizabeth saw a group of twelve men sitting in an open-planned thatch-roofed shed.

They were known as the wise men or the elders; as shown by their grey hair, and the furrows creasing their brows. Together, they formed the Council of Chiefs of Ikot Akara.

Elizabeth had known them her entire life.

They sat in a close circle – eleven of them on long bamboo benches. The twelfth chieftain, a tall imposing man in a long embroidery kaftan and black trousers, occupied a carved high-backed mahogany chair. On his head rested a woven black and white cap, with what looked to be the plume of an eagle wedged, slantwise, in one side.

He was their leader.

Despite their quiet murmurs, the gentle breeze of the early evening carried most of their words to her somber abode.

Soon after their arrival, one of the Chief's sons... she could not remember his name for the moment... an adolescent of about twelve, had brought in a keg of calabash filled with greyish white liquid; a tray with thirteen drinking gourds and a flat enamel plate, holding several large nuts. The boy had handed the plate of nuts to the leader who had then passed it on to the elder directly to his right. The second man broke the nuts into pieces and passed them back to the leader. The senior man took a piece and then nodded that the rest be distributed to the other Chiefs, and to a lone man sitting slightly outside their tight circle.

The young boy walked around the group, handing each man a drinking gourd and filling it with the palm wine.

When the ceremonial pouring of palm wine and the breaking of kola nut had been accomplished, the young boy bowed, excused himself and withdrew.

Before reconvening their discussion, the leader broke off a piece of his kola nut, chanted some words and then threw it on the ground; he followed that with a splash of wine from his gourd.

The spirit of their forefathers, whom the elders said was always present at every gathering, had been honoured.

'May it be so,' Elizabeth heard the rest of the elders respond in chorus.

But none took a bite off his kola or a sip from his wine. Instead, each chieftain held his piece of nut loosely in one fist and placed his full gourd on the floor beside his place on the long bench.

The wise men then brought their heads closer towards one another, murmured, and nodded solemnly in final agreement.

'Bring her in,' Elizabeth heard the leader command as he turned to the lone man sitting outside their circle.

He was much younger than the others – not more than twenty-four at most. He had been sitting with both arms wrapped tightly around his chest, giving the impression of wanting to be anywhere but among the circle of elderly men.

'We don't have all day, John,' said the leader a trifle harshly.

'Obong mi, please forgive me,' the youth said, uncurling hurriedly to his feet; 'my attentions walked away with my thoughts,' he said as he bowed in the direction of the head Chief, the man who was sitting in the very chair his own father had occupied barely three months before.

Elizabeth watched a couple of the elders pat John gently on the shoulder while the senior Chief contemplated his bowed head. Then he too gave the youth a reassuring pat before leaning down to murmur something into his ear.

The young man nodded and then stood upright once more.

Kukuruku... koo! The shrill crowing of a cockerel rent the air as he turned to walk away.

'Strange. That shadow says it's only a quarter to five. Why the crowing?' one of the elders asked no one in particular.

'The times are changing every day, my brother... before our very eyes,' another elder said. 'In my day, the noise of the cockerel was not heard until nigh on seven,' he shook his head sadly.

The shed where the meeting was held was commonly called an efe – the half walls put together with baked earth and polished to a high sheen with coals from leftover pieces of hard ebony wood. Clay drawings of animals adorned its walls. The efe was part of the senior Chieftain's compound, which comprised the main house, set about 200 yards away to the right, as well as smaller constructions belonging to the Chief's siblings and other members of his household. Over at the courtyard of the main house, subdued murmurings interspersed with kitchen clatter could be heard. The shed was where the head Chief and his council of elders judged cases brought to their attention.

Set well apart from all the other buildings was the compact hut where Elizabeth sat. John walked, head bowed and shoulders hunched, towards her.

'The rumours really must be true. Poor fellow. I hear he's almost an outcast in his own family,' one of the elders, Ita Sunday, whispered.

Another elder, The White One, because of his full head of woolly white hair, laid one hand hurriedly on the shoulder of the one who'd just spoken; with the other hand, he tapped his own lips and then pointed cautiously at John's departing back.

'A child is already born in the market square, before all and sundry, and you're still asking its mother to close her legs? What false modesty! And for what purpose?' Elder Ita Sunday said aloud in a truculent voice before shaking off his compatriot's hand.

'The worst kind of situation! Still, he is a man... he must behave like one, except for what's necessary,' said another of the wise men, buoyed by the defiant Elder Sunday.

'Terrible situation all around, tiffiiiaqua,' Elder Sunday spat dramatically over his shoulder.

'That it should happen to a him... a better man than his brother ever was, if I may say.'

'I agree there.'

Elizabeth listened as some elders continued to express their opinion, whilst others mulled over the predicament of the young man in silence.

The door of the hut clanged opened.

Elizabeth looked up.

I wonder why they sent him and not the guard, she thought.

'How're you, Lizzy? Were you able to sleep last night?'

Elizabeth said nothing.

'Again, you've eaten nothing today,' John said, looking at the untouched plate of food. 'Why won't you eat... even a little? Don't you like what is offered?'

Elizabeth glanced over at the full plate of soup, the oil already congealing along its surface and looked away.

'I've been requested by the elders to bring you,' John said and reached to help her up.

Elizabeth threw him a warning look and he stepped back.

61

'Why won't you let me help you, Lizzy?' The young man lowered his hand. 'How can anyone help you if you won't even help yourself? Please let me,' he lamented, but her face remained stony.

Poor John. How naïve he can sometimes, Elizabeth thought. When would he realize that this was a losing battle?

She stood upright, using the walls for support.

John moved forward to open the door. They emerged from the cabin and the door clanged shut again.

Elizabeth saw the wise men turn towards the sound.

Elizabeth tottered in front of John. She was young too, just a couple of years older than him. Light skin and a little plump, not fat and not entirely voluptuous – what the community referred to as 'nicely balanced.' She was dressed in a two-piece outfit Buba. Hers was made with a tie-die material of an indigo blue dotted with white flowers. The same piece of fabric covered her head, the ends knotted tightly at the nape of her neck. She stumbled with every step; each time the young man reached forward to help her, but she rebuffed his outstretched hands.

It took them almost ten minutes to walk the short distance from the hut to the efe. But she staggered forward with a straight back, head held high.

'Not exactly contrite, is she?' she heard an elder note.

Elizabeth stopped and speared him with her eyes. The man looked away hurriedly.

Eventually, she stood before them.

'Elizabeth. How're you? Were you served lunch today?' the Obong enquired.

Elizabeth stared straight ahead.

'There's a plate of food in the hut, my Lord, but it's untouched,' John answered.

'Why aren't you eating... is what you're given not to your liking? Tell me and I will have something else prepared for you.'

'Our family is grateful for your generosity and that of her Highness, Obong mi,' John interjected.

At the phrase *our family*, Elizabeth swiveled her eyes towards John. The younger man quailed at the look in them.

'Are you being treated fairly by your guard and those who bring your meals?' the leader persisted, despite her silence.

This pointless show of compassion; where was it when she had really needed it? The elders were, after all, not strangers to this village... they had known.

'Lizzy—' John prompted, reaching to grab her hand. Elizabeth jerked away. John's eyes reddened.

Elizabeth's heart softened for an instant; then it hardened again. She was done caring for anyone. Her emotions, the ones she had left, were now for her children: her daughters, seven-year-old Uyai, six-year-old Okuk, and their four-year-old brother, Anthony. When she thought of them, then and only then did she allow herself to feel. But she had learned to stifle that... even that.

Surely, John must know that she would never again be allowed access to her children? What kind of life did he think that would be for her?

She wished she had married him instead of his brother. But he'd been so young when she married Patrick: only thirteen years old to her eighteen, barely more than a child. That had not prevented him from following her around with doleful, besotted eyes. Most thought it quaint and took to calling him her second husband. It was only in jest... nothing scandalous.

'Elizabeth,' the leader said. He stopped to clear his throat several times. 'Lizzy,' he resumed. 'This has been the most difficult deliberation this council has ever had to undertake; however, the elders have arrived at a decision. Before we deliver it, is there anything you would like to say?'

Her daughters were safe, Elizabeth thought. The daughters would never have to walk through life carrying a terrible stigma, a shame to blight their every move. Then there was little Anthony...her sweet, sweet baby boy... something in Elizabeth's heart gave way as the face of her three-year-old boy flashed across her mind. That was another thing...

'Lizzy, His Royal Highness is speaking to you.'

'John, Elizabeth hears us. She can speak for herself,' The White One said.

'Oh, I was... was just... I just wanted...' the young man's voice trailed off miserably.

John had been her closest ally... her shield when his brother started hitting her less than a year into their marriage.

It began with what her mother-in-law termed 'love play' which left her with painful welts on her rump for days. Then it progressed to hard slaps on the face. Family members were called in several times and each time Patrick would say he loved his wife, vowing not to hurt her again.

But the promises were never kept.

Unlike their son, Patrick's people were kind to her. Most of Patrick's excesses were often curbed by the timely remonstrations of his parents.

As if an excuse were needed, John himself went out of his way to help his sister-in-law. A construction worker by trade, he ensured that the holes in her roof were sealed, the walls of her hut re-moulded and cemented; and when neessary, he would borrow a motorbike and transport her farm goods to the market, a job his brother, her husband, should have done.

'Stay for the family! One can see they care for you. Don't mind your husband, he will wake up to his responsibility one day,' Elizabeth's own family counseled.

Along the way, she lost her mother, and then gave birth to her own three children.

'You can't leave your children... who will care for them?'

Elizabeth did as she was advised.

A few days after her older daughter turned six, the beatings stopped as suddenly as it had started. For more than nine months Patrick did not batter her.

'I told you he would stop!' John was elated.

His mother lavished praises on her abusive son and took to calling Patrick her hero.

Yet here she was, standing in front of the elders.

One night, three months previously, she had been unable to sleep. She got up to check on the children. Anthony slept with his body curled like a shrimp on the bed Elizabeth shared with her husband. She pushed open the door to her daughters' room, and saw the head of her older daughter, Uyai, jerk up at the light coming in from the corridor.

'Mama!' the seven-year-old whispered.

Elizabeth froze.

Patrick's head jolted up and his eyes widened before he stood up and scurried pass her, back to their bedroom.

Elizabeth had rushed to her daughter after Patrick left the room. The little girl, eyes tearful, laid her head gently on her mother's shoulder.

'Mama are you angry with me? Did I do a bad thing?' She had whispered as Elizabeth dropped down and enfolded her in an embrace.

'No, my heart... I am not angry with you. Go to sleep, my heart...go to sleep,' Elizabeth had whispered back, unable to stop her own flow of tears.

'Then why are you crying? Papa said it was all right. He said it's a secret game all fathers play with their special daughter.'

'What're you talking about?' her husband had said nonchalantly the next morning as he side-stepped her to reach for a blue raffia bag he took to work every day. They were in the courtyard, behind their hut. Patrick was about to leave for his shop, where he sold building materials. The girls were in school and her mother-in-law had gone out, taking Anthony with her.

'Don't you pretend to me, Patrick! I saw! I saw!'

'Saw what? Can a man no longer tuck his own daughter into bed without all manner of insinuations?'

'Oh, my head! Spirit of my dead mother, come to my aid' Elizabeth had whispered, both arms placed on her head.

'Yeah, yeah, spirit of your dead mother... why don't you hurry up and join her,' Patrick jeered.

'I saw what I saw. I'm going to your father with this... don't think I'm stupid, Patrick!'

'Who will believe your stupid lies? My father is the Chief, the Paramount Ruler of this community, in case you have forgotten.'

How long had he been abusing their little girl... his own daughter? Was Uyai the only victim? Was he also touching Okuk? If not, how long before he turned on her too? Would anyone believe her? She wanted out! But her husband and his family would never allow her to take her children with her. How could she leave them behind knowing what might happen to them? On the other hand, how could she continue to stay under the same roof with such a man? Whatever she did the safety of her children was doomed with a man like Patrick as their father.

The thought was more than she could bear. Her eyes happened upon the axe used for wood chopping. It was leaning on the wall of the veranda. Without thinking, Elizabeth moved forward, picked it up and rounded on her husband.

Her husband screamed as the first blow caught him on the edge of the shoulder. The blood was warm on her face.

'Patrick! What's going on? I hope you're not beating that poor girl again?' His father's voice called out from the outhouse where he had gone to do his morning business.

Patrick reached for the axe but she was too quick for him. The otherworldly noise coming from his mouth caused his father to yell out again.

'Patrick! Patrick!' his father called out again. 'What's going on out there? Leave that girl alone! One of these days you will kill her and whatever sorrow comes from that you will carry with you all your life. I, Chief Linus Idoho, will not join in suffering the consequences of your madness.'

Her husband's screams were now a gurgle.

Again, the axe swung.

'Patrick, I say leave that girl alone… don't let me use this white hair on my head to curse you. You're trying my patience, boy!' The father's voice drew nearer, as he came out of the outhouse at a run. He rounded the corner, the front of his trousers held in both hands. He hadn't taken the time to pull the zipper.

He came to a stop at the scene before him.

His body twitched, his hands let go of the trousers and they dropped, gathering at his feet. At the same time, the old man leaned back and forth like a tree caught in a storm. He toppled and slowly folded on the dusty ground.

And still, Elizabeth kept hacking.

By now the neighbours had heard the commotion and were running towards the compound. They too came to a stop at the scene before them. Some tried to take the axe from her, but Elizabeth swung so widely that they stepped back in fear.

When at last she stopped, what was once her husband was now a pile of severed limbs and entrails. She herself stood, covered from head to toe in blood and gore, the bloodied axe dangling limply at her side.

When the dust finally settled there were two corpses: the mangled remains of her husband, and that of Elizabeth's father-in-law, who had had a heart attack and died right there on the spot where he collapsed.

It was a tragedy the likes of which the community had never before witnessed, or heard. And it divided them all, not just the immediate family of Chief Linus Idoho.

The police were brought in and quickly sent away.

'This is a family matter, we will deal with this as an internal matter,' declared the new Paramount Ruler. He had been quickly picked to help lead them to a decision about the outcome of the abomination that had contaminated their land.

Some pleaded for leniency on her behalf, pointing out the persistent abuse Elizabeth had suffered for years; others demanded harsh punishment.

Elizabeth's mother-in-law was among the latter.

'You set that killer free and all men in this community will forever be at risk at the hands of their wives. Is that what you want?' She challenged the Elders. 'An eye for an eye or I will deal with it myself.'

Elizabeth was transferred to the new Chief's compound to ensure her safety.

Among the Idoho clan, only John still maintained his affection for his sister-in-law.

While the debate raged, Elizabeth was silent. She had not uttered a word since her action.

Neither did she show remorse.

The few who felt sorry for her went to see her, begging her to show even a small sign of regret, enough to help in their clamor for mercy on her behalf.

Elizabeth maintained her silence.

So what if she lost her life? She thought as the small group meandered around her.

The world no longer held any appeal for her anyway. What mattered were her children: her daughters would never have to walk through life with the stigma of being raped by their own father... even under torture, she would never utter a word.

My girls are now safe. She repeated the mantra in her head as she stood now before the wise men. Little Anthony...

Her mind flinched again as the image of her baby son flashed upon it. What could she say to him later on in life if she was granted clemency? He was a boy after all; boys needed their fathers.

Despite the tenderness of her innermost thoughts, Elizabeth's face remained implacable.

'An eye for an eye,' the leader of the twelve wise men declared. 'That is your sentence. It will be carried out three days from now, on Afiong Eto market day, before sunlight, after the first crow of the cockerel.

'Obong mi... my fathers,' said John. His voice was desperate, spilling out the panic he had been trying to contain. 'Show mercy,' he pleaded. 'Lizzy is sorry... she wished she hadn't done this. She told me this herself when I went to fetch her. Tell them Lizzy!' he begged, turning to her. 'Tell His Royal Highness... our esteemed fathers here... how sorry you are... how you wished this never happened!'

Elizabeth turned her eyes on him once more. Poor, poor John. He could never understand. He probably thought her stupid, not to mention suicidal. But even to him, she could not divulge her secret. In their society, the stigma attached to sexual abuse trails a woman and affects all aspects of her life thereafter, and never for the good.

Imagine the entire community knowing that her daughter was raped by their father? Possibly even both of them? Her children's future would be permanently defaced, in peril. No! She could not risk that. Walls have ears, Elizabeth's mother used to say. The secret would be safe, locked in her grave. She had already made her Uyai promise never to reveal what her father had done. Not to anyone.

Her children were safe. It was what counted.

And little Anthony... he would never have to look into the face of the person who had deprived him of a father.

Wasn't that what love was supposed to be all about? To protect those you love, even if it means from your own self? No, she wasn't going to plead her case. It was better this way, Elizabeth decided.

She panned the faces of the elders present. Finally, squaring her shoulders and standing as straight as she possibly could, Elizabeth brought her unwavering stare back on their leader.

'I am not sorry,' she said.

THE old woman's voice fades as the story comes to an end. She even forgets to chant *Ekong nke-e*.

Esit-Ima is also silent. She covers her face with the palms of both hands and stays that way for a while. Silent. The old woman makes no effort to break the stillness. Eventually, Esit-Ima uncovers her face. Her cheeks are wet. Still, Nana says nothing.

'Why are human beings capable of such evil deeds, Nana? What takes place in the mind of a man who abuses his own daughter?'

The old woman remains silent. Finally, she looks up.

'I want you to make me a promise, my heart.'

'What, Nana?'

'Never be afraid to speak up against injustice, whether directed at you, at someone you know, or at someone you don't know.'

'Yes, Nana, you've told me that before.'

'I know, but it is worth repeating.'

'The elder did wrong, Nana. How could they make such a decision knowing she did what she did in self-defense? So she refused to apologize or show contrition? I am not sure I would have apologized either, Nana.'

'Tradition, my child. Tradition. We sanction the unspeakable in the name of tradition. Tradition should be for the people's betterment, men and women alike. Should it not honour and elevate, rather than subjugate and demean? Listen, my heart,' Nana lifts up Esit-Ima's chin and looks intently into her eyes. 'Any tradition, any at all, that does not uphold the rights of all members of its community, any tradition that says the rights of one part is of more importance that of the other parts, such a tradition should never be honoured.'

'What, then, do we do, Nana? What do we do against a custom that has become so deeply entrenched that it has become as unquestionable as, say, reaching for a cup of water when one is thirsty?'

'We must speak up, my heart. We must speak up... even if that's all we can do. Even if we are the lone voice, the only voice that does so. For when we fail to speak up against injustice and inequality, we give rise to more injustice and to greater inequality. Remember, my heart, the silence of those with a voice brings about the same effect to the growth of wickedness as water does to a field of plants. The silent voice of those who ought to speak up against evil promotes the increase of that same evil. Take the case of the Ibangas. They did not speak up. The abuse went on longer than it should have. Wife battering is the collective shame of an entire community, not just that of the victim upon whom it is perpetrated.'

'What about husband battering, Nana? I know it is **rare**, but what of women who abuse their husbands like Nkoyo, in Eboi?'

She is referring to an unusual case that took place a **year** before in a town not so far from theirs. A wife had locked her husband at the bottom of a dried-up unused well. She said he wasn't contributing to the upkeep of their home and five children, and that while he claimed not to have money, she had discovered that he had a secret family he was taking care of outside. The man was saved from what could have been an excruciating death when a passer-by heard his whimpering coming from inside the well. He had been locked in there for four days.

'Abuse is abuse, my heart, whether it is done by a man or a woman. It must all be condemned. Society must speak out against every and any form of abuse.'

'I understand now, Nana.'

Esit-Ima lays her head on the old woman's shoulder.

The next several days are busy ones as the Samsons prepare for the formal arrival of Esit-Ima's fiancé and his family. Esit-Ima herself had to always look her best, making it impossible for her to spend time with her Nana, or make the old woman's favourite drink or massage her feet, the two functions she has come to see as the most important service she could perform for her grandmother.

'Your Nana understands,' her mother comforts when Esit-Ima bemoans not being able to spend time with the old woman for several days in a row. They were in the kitchen peeling yams, ready to be pounded the following day.

'I know she does, Mother. Still....'

Her mother reaches forward to take the knife Esit-Ima has in her hand. 'Here, give me that,' she says. Then she pulls the tuber of yam from her daughter and lets it fall, thudding on the ground. 'Go!' she commands. 'Go to her.'

'But Mother, there's still so much to do for tomorrow, we have so many yams still to peel.'

Esit-Ima indicates the huge pile of unpeeled yams, even though they have already peeled so many.

'It's okay. Just go. I will get your cousins to come in and help. I hear voices. I believe some of them are around.'

'But Nana is having her afternoon rest. I won't disturb her from that.'

Esit-Ima's mother shakes her head. 'She is up already. I saw her head to the efe a few minutes ago.' Esit-Ima continues to hesitate, so her mother gets off her own stool, and pulls Esit-Ima from hers. 'Go!' she says.

The old woman is already comfortably ensconced among the cowhide futons, twiddling with the dials on her radio when Esit-Ima enters the efe. It is just past five o'clock and the news of the hour is in progress.

'The monsoon deluge in India has already claimed many lives, including those of young children... Twenty-seven year-old Khushi Arjun lost her three-year-old daughter in the ensuing flood that has carried off half the buildings in her community...'

The old woman is so engrossed in what she is doing she doesn't respond to Esit-Ima's 'Good day, Nana, hope you rested well?' Esit-Ima repeats the greeting and the old woman lifts her left hand and waves at her without looking up. Esit-Ima had stopped by her Nana's room to pick up the lotion for the old woman's massage. She opens the jar of lotion and scoops out a dollop. Nana's feet are already stretched out. Esit-Ima lathers them as usual and begins to knead in a gentle circular motion.

Both women concentrate on what they are doing for a while, Nana at her radio, which is still detailing the effects of the monsoon in India, and Esit-Ima at her massage.

The news comes to an end and Nana turns to her grand-daughter. 'I will tell you a story of a different kind today, my heart, one that holds a vital lesson.'

'I am listening, Nana' she says.

'This one is extremely important,' the old woman insists.

Esit-Ima looks up, smiling. 'I am listening, Nana,' she says again.

'Ekong nke-e.'

'*Nke ekong Abasi. Ekong aka, ekong oyong, ekong isi maha udim.*'

Papa Brought Home a Catfish

I BROUGHT the pestle down on the television. 'Cheating, lying...bastard! Let's see what you and your latest heartthrob will watch now,' I screeched.

The Bang Olufsen television screen refused to shatter. Instead, it got all spidery – like a tarred road disturbed by a seismic eruption. I wasn't letting that stop me. I continued to smash my soon-to-be-ex-boyfriend's most prized possession with the pestle I'd taken from the kitchen. As hot tears streamed down my cheek, I spied something scurry from beneath the table on which the television was now weaving back and forth. A cockroach. Fat and healthy-looking; its wings a perfect deep golden-brown color. I turned, lifted a foot and stamped down hard...and missed. Instead, my leg hit a pod-shaped side-stool loaded with the latest magazines on design and technology, another crazy passion of Solomon's. Glossy magazines spilled in every direction. From the periphery of my vision, I saw the roach scamper away. I had come back earlier that morning, after four days away on a business trip that was supposed to have lasted a week. Thinking to surprise my boyfriend, I'd stopped by the market to get ingredients for a lamb dish I'd seen prepared by a celebrity cook on television. I had the spare keys he'd given me, so rather than do the cooking at my place and carrying it over, I decided to prepare the meal at his apartment.

The first thing I saw when I stepped through the door was a white linen blouse carelessly draped over one of the dining room chairs. It was too flimsy to belong to his mother. His younger sister, Janet, the only other person who could own such a garment, was away at school and not expected back home on holiday until the end of the following month. Bewildered, I picked up the blouse to examine it.

The second thing that hit me was an appetizing aroma wafting from the kitchen. Balling up the blouse, which smelled faintly of cocoa butter, I walked towards the kitchen. Tentative, I pushed open the door; and saw it. A shiny, new silver-pot smack in the centre of the gas cooker; its cover slightly tipped to the side.

I felt queasy, as my boyfriend was not the kind of guy who goes out to buy new pots. Opening the lid, I found the pot brimming with fish stew. Strips of scent-leaves peeped out of what I realized were chunks of red snapper – the most sought-after fish in town. My chest heaved. This was not Solomon's handiwork. Solomon couldn't cook a stew like that in a month of Sundays. It had the hallmark of a girl trying very hard to please her new man. Fish! I recoiled. I stared at hunks of the slippery creature. Pacing back and forth in the kitchen, my mind went back to the months of happiness we'd shared.

We first met at the check-out counter of one of the leading supermarkets in Victoria Island in Lagos. I was rummaging inside my handbag for my ATM card, after realizing that the cash I had was not enough to pay for my groceries. Frazzled and feeling slightly embarrassed, I had been about to snap 'Be patient' at the cashier's constant 'Madam, please, we have many customers waiting,' when someone behind me handed an ATM card to the woman and said, 'Put it on my card.'

Turning around to thank my savior, and to assure him that I would return his 7,300 Naira to him as soon as we stepped out and found the nearest cash point, I encountered the friendliest of smiles from a light-skinned man of average height. He was in his early to mid-thirties and was dressed in shorts and a polo shirt. His skin had a sweaty sheen as if he'd just stepped out of the gym.

'Don't worry about it,' he said, outside the supermarket. He refused my bank card, which I had now found and was furiously waving it at him to assure him of my genuine intention to return his money.

'You're so kind, but I have to give back your money,' I replied, then hurriedly added, 'I don't mean to seem ungrateful but I will feel extremely uncomfortable if you don't take it.'

'In that case, buy me a drink with it,' he responded, handing me his business card. 'Later this evening, if you have time. I would really like that,' he added, bathing me with another of his warm smiles.

We met that evening. I was prepared this time, taking along 20,000 Naira, but at the end of the evening, he insisted on paying the bill.

'Hold on to it and buy me dinner tomorrow,' he said when I protested. For the next two weeks, it became his standing joke. We went out five times. On each occasion, he would refuse my offer to pay the bills and instead suggest another dinner, another drink, or another lunch date. After three months together, he suggested another kind of date – lunch with his parents.

'This is the one,' he smiled, bashful at his mother's rivers of inquiries.

Had that been a lie? The pot of fish told me that it was. 'If I am really the one, why cheat on me before we've even started?'

Remembering that first meeting at his parent's home, my chest twisted, and I felt a bitter taste in my mouth. I heaved the pot from the stovetop. It clattered, a crashing cacophony on the tiled floor. Pieces of fish flew everywhere. I looked down at the blouse still balled up in my fist. Shaking it open, I held it out with both hands and ripped it from collar to hem. Then I stamped the offending fabric into the puddles of soup streaming across the kitchen floor.

'Fish... again?' I spat, my anger in no way dissipated by the carnage.

For reasons I have never been able to understand, the cataclysmic events in my love life have always been associated with these glassy-eyed, slippery creatures. Until I met Solomon, fish had haunted my love life like remembered scenes from a nightmare.

I was twelve years old, and it was a late afternoon in the harvest season. My father brought home the biggest catfish the village of Ikot Asian had ever seen. Papa loved his family and delighted in springing surprises and treats on us. In those days, no treat pleased us children more than a deliciously-prepared rice dish, with meat or fish in abundance. In our home, we children all ate out of one communal bowl or tray. It was, therefore, a huge treat when my siblings and I got served our own individual plates. Even better was when the portions were enough to satisfy each child. This ensured that the older children wouldn't resort to stealing the younger ones' portions, a frequent occurrence in a polygamous home made up of two wives and eleven children. As was usual during harvesting season, everyone on the farm had brought back produce from the fields. Harvest work included helping to stack yams in the dry enclave built especially for them, or fetching water from the stream to sustain the constant drinking, bathing, and cooking. Harvest was a trying, tiring time, but it was also a fun and happy season in the lives of all the farmers in our village. Our family was no exception. For that reason, Papa went out of his way to offer unusual incentives to his family as well as the farmhands and day laborers who were paid to come in and help. It was his way of showing appreciation for all our hard work. My father was known for treating his family and workers with a level of love and dignity that was uncommon amongst other farmers, even for miles around.

On that hot afternoon in August, Papa brought home three big catfish. And a boy. We were in the lean-to shack we used as the kitchen. It must have been somewhere around five-thirty in the evening because the sun was just beginning to bid goodbye to our village.

It was the first time I laid eyes on Edem. The first time I fully understood the word, man. And the first time I knew fully what it meant to want one.

I could only wonder how a man could be that beautiful. He was about eighteen; tall and lanky, with the softest curly-black hair, like that of a new-born baby. His skin was like ebony, with such a shine to it that looked as if he had just taken a bath, and finished it with a jar of Vaseline petroleum jelly. When he smiled a 'thank you' for the cup of water my little sister Ima had given him, his eyes gleamed pure white against his dark skin. He was only too aware of the effect he was having on the young female members of our family, who had all come out to see the fish Papa had brought home. 'This is Edem, fisherman Ekpo's eldest son,' said Papa, explaining the presence of the beautiful stranger with him. 'He lives with his uncle in Lagos and has just been admitted into a University there to study Engineering. Very kind of him, offering to help bring the fish on his father's motorcycle,' he added, turning to smile at the boy.

'Lord in the bright sky!' My mother and stepmother exclaimed in unison; then they walked around the boy, cooing in admiration.

'You must be Madet's first son,' my mother said. 'Yes, Ekamba Mma,' the boy smiled and bowed his head, a form of respect when addressing those who were older. He also addressed Mama as 'Big Mother,' another sign of honour.

'I knew your face was familiar!' my mother clicked two fingers on her right hands, pleased to have arrived at the right conclusion. 'You were this tall the last time I saw you,' she added, indicating with her left hand a height just above her knee.

'Yes, Ekamba Mma,' the boy smiled and bowed again.

'You can't mean that this is Madet Ekpo's son? Isn't he the same boy I saw two years ago at his sister's betrothal?' my stepmother asked.

'Yes, Mma.' Edem answered, tilting his head, this time in the direction of my stepmother.

'The amazing way children grow once they are out of the

womb. A boy yesterday, now he is taller than all of us combined,' my mother said.

'May I please have more water?' the boy asked, waving the cup towards my little sister, who was busy flicking droplets of water off her arm.

My mother rounded on her. 'Go get Edem more water, Ima! Can't you see he would like some more? Why are you standing there gawping as if the good Lord has taken away your common sense?'

'Ask me what they are staring at!' my stepmother said because by this time three of her daughters, in addition to myself (and of course Ima, my little sister, who had been sent to get the water) had strolled over to gape at the beautiful boy.

'And why are you all out here?' my stepmother continued, 'who is watching the peeled cassava so the goats don't get at it?'

'Go bring me a basin of water to wash my hands,' Papa instructed one of my siblings. And Mmayen, get a chair for the young man,' Papa said, turning to me. 'Where are your manners, young lady?'

'Do I know?' my stepmother interjected again. 'Teach children from morning until night falls and the moment a visitor steps in, they shame you by behaving as if you haven't taught them a single thing.'

'Mmwwssph,' my mother puckered her lips and let out a huge hiss of in support.

I stood, still too enraptured to go on my errand.

'Did you hear your father?' Mother snapped, bringing my mind back from a dream of a traditional betrothal between Edem and me.

'Yes,' I responded.

'Yes what, Mmayen Ekanem Inua?' Mother tended to call us by our full name whenever she was angry, or frustrated.

'Yes, Papa, Mma' I responded, bowing, my knee slightly bent. This was the female's equivalent of Edem's head bowing.

'Aniekan! Aniekan Ekanem Inua!' she began calling for my fourteen-year-old sister as I went off to get the stool.

'Where is your sister?' she demanded when I brought back the chair.

'She went to the river-side garden to pick greens for supper, Mother.'

'Oh, I'd forgotten about that, Nene,' her voice taking on a conciliatory tone.

Nene was Mother's special name for me. Because I was born the same night her grandmother passed away, Nene was her term of endearment. She believed her grandmother had come back to her in the form of a daughter. 'Anyway, why are you here? You were supposed to go with her,' she said.

'May I wait a little while before I go, Mother, please?' I pleaded, tentative, taking advantage of her mellowed tone. I wanted to linger in the presence of our guest.

'Why? Why do you want to go in a little while... are you incubating eggs right now?' she asked, her brows furrowing afresh in annoyance. 'Look at the sun, will it refuse to fall into the sea just to give you time to make up your mind?'

'Pfff, pfiff, pfiff,' she spat dramatically on the ground. 'If you are not at the farm helping your sister before this spit dries up, you will see the color of my red eyes, for the next three days, at the very least.'

Taking the wooden stool from me, she placed it in a shady spot by the verandah. Then she took Edem gently by the hand and helped him onto the stool.

'And close your mouth,' she clucked, as I prepared to depart from the compound to do her bidding. 'It's unbecoming for a girl your age to leave her mouth hanging open that way.'

As I walked by, I caught Sandra's mischievous looks and heard her muffled giggles. She was the least favourite of all my stepsiblings because she was forever devising means to try to get me into Father's bad books.

Up until that point, if anyone wanted to upset me, all they had to do was threaten to marry me off. I would wail and scream for hours. But for the first time in my young life, the idea of marriage did not seem quite so barbaric. With that thought snaking through my befuddled mind, I began my first fantasy of what it might be like between a man and a woman.

Every dream I had from then on was of Edem. In my head, I would encounter him at the stream and, somehow, it would always just be the two of us. Edem would then go to beg Papa for my hand in marriage. I even dreamed of finding a sick Edem lying by the side of the road, and rescuing him. In gratitude, of course, he would declare his love and devotion to me.

My dreams took a surreal turn; I dreamed of him at my desk in school, while assisting at the farm, or buying crayfish for Mother at the market; I even saw his face mirrored in my ball of fufu at meal times. To compound my situation, I took to becoming the family's errand runner, something I used to do anything to avoid. Now I went to great lengths to ensure I would be sent on any errand that would result in meeting

Edem. Even just seeing him made me happy. Buying kerosene for cooking no longer meant a battle between my sisters and me about 'who bought it the last time.' The kerosene depot was two houses away from the Ekpo's compound. I was willing to help buy kerosene for our entire community if it meant seeing him for even just a second.

Barely two weeks later, I had tied myself into such a knot over him that I became physically ill. The man of my dreams seemed blissfully unaware of my fawning adoration. Until one afternoon, three weeks after Papa brought home the fish. I had been on another kerosene errand and was half a mile from home when I saw Edem standing by the wild Udara tree on the last corner before the final stretch to our home.

'Hey, Mmayen. How are you?'

I'd been praying for such a moment. Now that it was happening, my mouth went dry. I could not utter a single word.

'You're looking very pretty today. Where're you coming from?'

Pretty, he called me pretty! I grabbed at those sweet words as I watched him leave the tree and walk towards me.

'I went, ummm...mmmm, I went to get some kerosene for Mma, for Mama Isaiah,' I mumbled.

'Mama Isaiah, that's your stepmother, right?' I nodded affirmation.

'That's kind; what a nice girl you are. Can I walk you home?' he asked, and joined me before I could respond.

We had been walking for a few minutes, with him talking and me generally mumbling and harrumphing like an old woman with a throat disease, when he suddenly stopped and asked,

'Mmayen, can I ask you to do something for me, please?'

Thinking he wanted to ask if he could call on me, I mumbled. 'Yes, of course, anything.'

Pulling a folded brown envelope from his pocket he pointed it towards me.

'Can you give this to your sister, Sandra, for me please?'

'Sa...Sand...Sandra?' I garbled, as it dawned on me that he had waylaid me because he wanted a messenger to run between him and Sandra, my fifteen-year-old stepsister. Sandra, my least favourite stepsibling; Sandra, who was always trying to get me into trouble with Papa; Sandra, who poked fun at me at every turn and referred to me derisively as The Cloud Dweller because our family said I tended to walk around as if I was permanently in a dreamland. Sandra... Sandra... Sandra. At that moment, I hated my tall, coquettishly beautiful stepsister with every fibre of my being.

'Please don't let anyone else see that. Sandra says she trusts you... that you're her favourite sister,' he added as he pressed the brown envelope into my limp palm. Sandra trusts me? Me, her favourite sister? Bearing in mind how she had always treated me, this added insult to an already stinging injury. Nodding 'yes' to his repeated pleas, I scurried away. I was desperate to get away from him. The knowledge that my first love wanted my half-sister instead of me sent me into such a funk of misery that I became ill. No amount of my Mother's castor oil mixed with bitter herbs – a foul concoction she swore cured every known and unknown malady – could resolve my particular ailment; nor could a trip to the only clinic in the area. My poor family was perplexed.

'Tell me, my Heart. Is it food? Don't you like what I've been preparing, Ebebe? Just tell me, and I will get you whatever you want,' my mother cajoled.

I refused to tell her what the problem was, preferring to deal with the first major rejection of my young life in private. Instead, I developed a strong aversion to fish; which was a pity because, being from the Niger Delta region, fish was our main source of protein.

The next time my heart was bruised by fish was during an inter-house sports event in my final year at high school. This time the object of my affections was the captain of our rival athletic team. My antenna should have blinked 'fishy' when I walked into the cavernous school cafeteria and found him chomping on a plateful of Saint Christopher's Friday Special, deep-fried mackerel and tomato stew with steamed yam. I had gone in to get a bottle of water to freshen up, in preparation for the four-hundred-meter sprint in which I was competing. Our schools were age-old rivals for the plaque known as the Young Warriors Trophy, which had been going back and forth between them for as long as they'd been in existence. Once we got to know each other, he had promised to 'love me forever.' That is, until he got the attention of a girl in my year whose father was rumoured to be the next contestant for the State's governorship. Needless to say, his desire to be intimately connected to such a family trumped the 'endless love' he'd promised me for the last six months.

'What the hell's wrong with men?' I mumbled, coming a little to my senses as I took in the chaos I had created in Solomon's sitting room. 'Give them your heart, your time, your energy, cook their favourite meal, iron their shirts, pander to their annoying relatives, and generally wear yourself out anticipating their every pleasure. And what do you get for all your pain? A lying, cheating, no good scoundrel! Before I am done, he'll know never to cheat on a good woman. Or a bad one for that matter.' My laughter was tinged with mania.

Then I heard the keys in the front door. It was only three-thirty in the afternoon. Solomon never got back from work until well into the evening. That could only mean one thing. I jumped to my feet in anticipation.

'Let it be the bitch who cooked that soup,' I mumbled, reaching for the pestle. I had the stomach for a fight.

I struggled upright, the pestle at the ready. I didn't know what I was prepared to do, but it was going to be something, that's for sure.

'Mmayen! You're back!'

The air whooshed from my lungs as the petite frame of Janet, Solomon's younger sister, waltzed in through the door, holding a plastic-covered package in her left hand.

'Janet!' I cried. 'What are you doing here?'

'Nice way to welcome your future sister-to-be,' Janet replied, eyebrows raised at my abrupt tone. She was carrying a parcel. She held it up proudly. 'I arrived early this morning... I decided...' her voice tailed off and she gasped. 'Oh my God! What happened here?' Her mouth formed a big round 'O' at sight of the mess in the sitting room.

'The fish... you're not supposed to be here. You're supposed to be at school...' I muttered stupidly, dropping the pestle. The loud clatter, as it landed on the floor, caused the younger girl to step back, startled.

Then as her eyes took in the pestle and its still reverberating sound, comprehension dawned.

'Oh, Mmayen! What in God's name have you done?' she wailed, her eyes following the trail of liquid to the kitchen. 'Oh my God, I bought that fish this morning at Market Junction,' Janet stopped and raised her palm to her opened mouth. She stared, wide-eyed, at the pieces of cooked fish scattered about the floor. 'I made snapper stew for Solo. As a surprise.' She pointed at the empty pot. 'I bought that pot this morning.' She looked around the room, aghast. Then she saw the blouse. She picked it up. 'This is also mine,' she said. 'Some of the fish juice splattered on it, so I changed before I went out to market. It's one of my favourites.' Her voice was full of reproach. In a daze, she wandered into the sitting room, still carrying the blouse. I heard a sharp inhalation of breath as she took in the TV. She ran her hand delicately back and forth over the shattered screen.

The immensity of what I'd done hit me then, like a wedge of an ice making its way slowly down my gullet to my stomach. 'Janet, I'm done for,' I whimpered. 'He'll never forgive me for this. Oh God, what have I done? I've lost him... oh, I have lost him good and proper for sure.'

'Solo loves you. Matter of fact, he's crazy about you, Mmayen. Why didn't you wait? Why didn't you confront him face-to-face if you thought he was cheating on you?' Arms akimbo, the plastic parcel still in her left hand.

Her question hung in the air, mocking me, taunting me. Because what could I say? I'd never even thought of that. I couldn't think, not with the rage I'd been feeling.

'Goodness!' Janet exclaimed as the heel of one of her shoes crushed a piece of glass. The noise galvanized me into action. I went down on all fours.

90

'Janet, please, help me,' I pleaded as I struggled to pick up pieces of fish, glass shards and torn bits of paper.

'You smashed his stuff, Mmayen! Has he ever given you cause for jealousy, to be suspicious?"

'No!' I wailed. 'You have to understand what it looked like when I walked in here! A strange woman's blouse! A dish cooking away, all the hallmarks of a romantic meal for two... Janet, I have less than two hours to buy a new television, please help me!'

I scuttled over to lie prostrate in front of Solomon's sister as the clock on the metal cabinet struck four. It was humiliating, but I was past caring.

'Mmmmm,' was all I received from the girl who would have been my sister-in-law in less than a year.

'Jan, please. He must never find out what I've done. Say something, please,' I begged.

'What do you want me to say, Mmayen? Really... what?'

'Will he ever forgive me? Why didn't I wait... why didn't I just wait? For once in my life... oh, my God, oh, my head, I have ruined my chance of love forever. It was the fish... that fish... the sight of that fish.' Solomon's sister did not respond. But the look on her face said it all. It was the expression of someone watching another who she thought was completely deranged.

Then the young girl turned toward the coffee table littered with torn magazines and threw the plastic bag she'd been holding onto it.

The bag split open on landing, and a large catfish flopped out.

'*Ekong nke-e.*'

'*Nke ekong Abasi.* You were right Nana, this one was special.' As she has done on several occasions, Esit-Ima leans forward and hugs the old woman. 'Thank you,' she says.

The old woman beams at her. 'I am glad. You do know why I had to tell you this one, don't you?'

'I do, Nana. I really do. What terrible, terrible havoc jealousy can cause. And it starts off usually so simply. Do you think Solo ever found out about Mmayen's destruction of his things? If he did, did he forgive her?'

'Would you?' Nana throws the question right back at Esit-Ima.

'I don't know, Nana. But if he truly loved her the way the story tells us he did, then he ought to, no? True love always forgives.'

'Yes, my heart, but even the most loving person finds it hard to deal with lack of trust.'

'Mmmm, marriage, Nana, I am beginning to wonder whether I am ready for it.'

'True, my heart, marriage is not a journey for the faint of heart, even with deep love. But you will be okay. I know you will be okay,' the old woman pats Esit-Ima lightly on the back.

'No one wants to start on such a journey knowing their partner does not trust them, I know that Nana. Still, I feel so sorry for Mmayen. Fate seems to have played against her, there were indications that her suspicions were grounded, yet…'

'Again, true. Anyway, this is not about Mmayen, but about you. What would you have done in Mmayen's shoes? If every piece of seemingly factual evidence pointed to the conclusion that Benjie was cheating on you, what would you have done?'

'Nana...' Esit-Ima begins then stops. 'Nana, I...' she says again. Again, she stops. His face bunches up in concentration. The old woman watches her, deep, rheumy eyes unflinching as she focuses them on Esit-Ima. The two lock eyes. Esit-Ima is the first to look away. 'Nana, I...'

'You don't know, do you?' the old woman says gently.

Esit-Ima nods, 'I don't know,' she admits.

'And that is okay, my heart. Silence. That is the key to a crisis-free life. When you don't know, when you are not sure, despite seemingly obvious clues, simply do nothing. Never take an action unless you are absolutely sure. Even then, choose the wise route of silence. It will calm your heart. True silence will calm your heart. For only in the deep calmness of the heart, where peace dwells, only there can wise decisions be found. For like water to a raging fire, so is silence to a raging tongue. It stays the hand and prevents evil from marching forth.'

'Ekong nke-e.'

'Nke ekong Abasi. Ekong aka, ekong oyong, ekong isi maha udim.'

Secrets of the Dark

WHEN her daughter died at the tender age of seventeen, Grandma Liz, in her grief, seized upon the only thing that gave her comfort at the time – naming me. She wanted the honour of christening the child her daughter had managed to bring into the world after three days of labor before taking her last breath. Grandmother chose Idongesit-mi, which literally means, my only comfort, an apt name, under the circumstances.

Watching my granny scoop a handful of dry crayfish from an old Bournvita can into a small wooden mortar, I wonder how my life would have turned out if my mother had lived. Certainly not the way it changed sixteen years ago, when I was only eleven. And it most certainly would not have featured Pastor Joshua as the principal player.

'They're going to see your father tomorrow,' Grandma Liz tells me. As if I didn't already know.

'Yeah, I know,' I say, and reach to drag forward a plate containing a small plastic bag of salt.

'They're a good and decent family… hard working, and kind to their womenfolk,' she leans to stay my hand, forcing me to look at her. 'They are, you know,' she says, referring to the James family, who was going to see my father the next day to ask for my hand in marriage to their son, Ita.

94

'Mmmm' I mutter again and then begin picking imaginary lint out of the salt.

'Why are you so uninterested?' she leans closer, staring deep into my eyes, her brow furrowed and eyes narrowed.

Why are seemingly innocent people capable of the most atrocious evil, I want to ask.

'He no longer has any power over you, if that's your fear,' she caresses the skin just beneath my thumb, sensing the reason for my lack of interest.

I look at her gentle, weather-beaten face.

'It's that great-grandchildren issue again, isn't it, Nne?' I say instead, putting on the jovial tone I was now used to adopting whenever the issue of marriage, my marriage, comes up.

'Don't!' she says, making me feel guilty for trivializing a topic that obviously means so much to her. I lean over to give her a hug. 'Don't worry, I will give you a great-grandchild soon,' I promise.

'When?' my grandmother raises one eyebrow.

'When the right man comes along.'

'Right man? Is he to be dropped from the heavens, this 'right man?' You have had suitors… and all things considered… in numbers, many young girls in this village would give their breath for; yet you have rejected them all. Let's hope you won't reject this one,' she adds, with a hint of desperation in her voice.

'Nne, can we not talk about this now, please? It's not the right time for…'

'When will it ever be the right time? The stars in your womb will not keep their torch burning forever just for you.'

Stars-burning-in-the womb was Grandma Liz's' reference to women who were not too old to conceive.

The stars in her womb have long dimmed, she would say of women well past their menopause.

'I am not that old, Gran-gran!' I bump her shoulder playfully as I use my pet name for her.

'Not that old!' she scorns, turning her gaze upon me, with brows again lifted. 'Your cousin Ido is twenty-four and the baby in her womb is her second. Come next planting season, you'll be twenty years plus eight planting seasons...'

'Nne, I know well enough that I am turning 28 soon, no need to remind me. If I've rejected all my suitors to-date it's because they were not right for me,' I snap. It pained my heart to see the look of hurt surprise on her face.

'I am so sorry, Nne. I meant no disrespect.'

Reaching out, I pull the stalk of greens she is picking for the evening dinner from her hands, drop it in the basket in front of her and hold her work-worn hands in mine. Sweat dots her face, plastering some of her grey-streaked hair along her forehead. I reach up and brush the hair gently aside.

Life has not been too kind to my Grandma Liz. The third wife in a polygamous marriage, her husband passed away when her first and only child was just five. That child had, in turn, passed away a little over twelve years later while trying to give birth to me. Grandma Liz's hair turned white overnight; she was still a few years short of forty when it happened. Grandma, herself has only one sibling – a brother – who she barely sees, because he lives with his own family in Onitsha, a teeming market town 500 kilometers away from our village. I understand her need for great-grandchildren, and for me to have a family of my own. If only I could overcome my fear, I think to myself.

'I'm not insensitive to all you've been through, Adiaha-ima, but I am concerned for you,' she says, her voice breaking over the special name she uses for me. Adiaha-ima means beloved first daughter. She uses it more than my formal name.

In our culture, a name is considered very thoroughly because it has to echo the heart and emotion of the parents of the child. More often than not it is linked to a wish, praise, a promise, a thanksgiving, or a petition to God; and is usually given by the father of the child.

Mine was one of the few exceptions.

Grandmother picks up a pestle and begins to ground the crayfish.

'I know your turmoil, Adiaha-ima. Don't think I am insensitive,' she says, amid the pom-pom-pom sound of the pestle striking the mortar. 'Who will look out for you when I am gone if you don't get married? Even had you wished to return to your father's household, he and his wife are more concerned with their own problems.'

She was referring to my stepmother's frequent miscarriages and the fact that she hadn't been able to carry a pregnancy to term since the birth of her first child, my half-sister, Abasi-ama.

'I'll be fine, Nne,' I say, hugging her tight again. 'Papa and Aunt Mafiong are not my only living relatives; have you forgotten Aunty Emilia?'

'Ah, yes, Emilia... may the good Lord bless that child. Still, she does have her own issues, too... that husband of hers! More and more that man is living in his palm-wine calabash... what passes for men these days!' she harrumphs.

Aunt Emilia is Papa's only sister and she's married to a palm-wine tapper. According to concerned whispers in our community, more than half of the wine my aunt's husband taps ends up inside his ever-growing belly rather than on the shelf of his kiosk.

'I am starving!' I jump up from the stool and walk over to open the earthenware pot bubbling on the stove. 'By the time this soup is ready I'll be so old and ugly no man will give me a single glance,' I squish up my face and mimic the stumbling steps of the very old.

'Don't you dare touch my pot!' my grandma feigns anger. 'You should never open another woman's cooking pot without her permission; haven't I taught you anything, child?' Walking over, she takes the lid gently from my hand and replaces it back over the pot. Turning around, she lays one calloused hand on my cheek.

'You? Ugly? Never! You're exactly like your mother. My Nsima. Even at a young age, no man could walk by without taking a second look.'

'Can I ask a question, Nne?'

'Of course, Idongesit-mi,' she pats the back of my hand.

'Why are the value of women in our society counted only in our ability to marry and the number of children we bear?'

'That's a strange question, Idongesit. Are you saying it's wrong for women to get married, or bear children?'

'No, Nne. It just seems that whatever we do, however hard we try, our worth is never acknowledged unless we have a husband, and children.'

'I appreciate how hard you've worked to grow your palm-oil business, my dear,' she begins... choosing to address my concerns in her own peculiar meandering way. 'Just the other day, Emilia was saying that in your father's village your name is now the by-word for hard work and good business sense; that, in fact, every mother wants her daughter to be like you. As for having children... it's a good thing, Adiaha-ima. The good Lord made it so,' she hastens to add, giving me the answer I knew she would.

'How about marriage, then, Nne?'

'That too is from the good Lord, and it can be good.'

'What happens when it isn't?'

'Why are we dwelling on this topic, Adiaha? Are you afraid? You shouldn't be... Ita James is a good boy from a great family.'

Giving me a look of mischief she adds, 'To be sure, he's not the tallest man you've ever seen. But he's good and decent, nonetheless. And so are his parents.'

The face of Pastor Joshua flashes across my brain.

'It's not that bad, Adiaha,' Grandma Liz laughs, misinterpreting my sigh. 'There's more to a man than height, you know. Moreover, despite his small stature he's still handsome, and virile too, so I have heard,' she gives me a sly look from under her lashes as she heaps a spoonful of ground crayfish into the steaming pot on the fire.

'Virile? What has that got to do with being good?' I ask.

'Just saying, my dear.'

As she goes about preparing dinner I look at her bent back – if only she knew. The thought of myself in a room at night with a man - albeit one to whom I am married - terrifies me. The thought of that man being big and virile sends me into a panic. It's been that way since the night Aunt Emilia dropped me off at Pastor Joshua's home.

Jovially called the roving pastor because he rejected the notion of belonging to one particular church body, Pastor Joshua was an enigma in our community – more so because when it came to religious affiliation, ours was a community that believed in the importance of 'picking a route, and staying on it.'

A fiery and charismatic preacher, his sermons were infused with humour and elaborate use of metaphor. For this reason, he was invited to preach in many Pentecostal churches in our community.

'I am the Lords' servant; called to do His work whenever He wants and wherever He wants. I can't be restricted or confined by conventions,' he would say when some of those churches attempted to make him their permanent preacher.

Tall and slight of build, with a permanent expression of surprise – as if he'd just missed a step on a flight of stairs – he had a sharp angular face, dewy eyes, and full soft lips, like that of a young girl. 'A beautiful face,' some said; which was why most people were surprised he was still single at thirty – the age where most men in our community were long married and had fathered multiple children.

'No time! No time!' he would say when pressed about it.

Pastor Joshua was also known to be a great philanthropist and very forward-looking. When not sermonizing about the second coming, his frequent mantra was 'Educate the female child, she's the backbone of our future.'

At most gatherings, his was the lone voice that spoke out for women, the only one striving to right the inequality prevalent in our society. As a result, other men called him Woman Wrapper behind his back.

A wrapper is a piece of fabric worn by women in our society and is as vital to the wardrobe of women from our culture as a dress is to the wardrobe of a Western woman. A woman wrapper is a man believed to be under the thumb of the womenfolk in his life. To be referred to as such constitutes an enormous insult, but if Pastor Joshua knew of this derogatory name he showed no concern.

'A man who does not honour his womenfolk does not deserve honour himself. Quote me anytime,' he would re-iterate in the presence of the same men who called him names.

In a society that valued male children above female, and where access to higher education is most likely to favour the former rather than the latter, it was no surprise that his magnanimous views earned him love and respect among the women of his community.

When I was eleven, Pastor Joshua chose my cousin, Ini, who was a year older than me, to serve him. Within a few weeks, Ini was sending desperate messages that she wanted to return home. When asked why she did not want to stay with the Pastor, even though he had sent her straight away to school and bought her a nice new uniform, plus sandals and school bag (which were the envy of those who were in her class), she had responded...

'I just want to go home.'

Besides the offer of education, it was said that Pastor Joshua had also agreed to pay my cousin's mother two thousand Naira every month.

'To compensate for all the help she gives you in your household,' the Pastor had said, in response to her mother's profuse gratitude.

'What a good and thoughtful man,' my stepmother said when she learned of Pastor Joshua's kind gesture. 'How foolish to lose such an opportunity... what's wrong with Atim's daughter?' she complained to my father the day Ini was brought back from the Pastor's village. 'I wish I had a daughter old enough to send,' she'd added.

That was when they hit on the idea of sending me. As I said, I was only eleven.

When the day came to depart I was sad to leave the only place I'd ever known.

'Why so gloomy, Idongesit?' Aunt Emilia had tried to comfort me as we made our way down the forest path to Pastor Joshua's.

I opened my mouth to answer, but no sound came out.

'This is a wonderful opportunity for you. You get to go to school, as you've always wanted,' she added, taking my hand and drawing me close to her side.

'Why didn't Ini want to stay, Aunty?'

'Ah, so that's why you are worried! Ini doesn't like being away from home. She's the only child of her mother, as you know. Always been a Mama's girl, that one. Anyway, her loss is your gain, my dear.'

'But she came back so sad.'

'Yes, I agree. That was strange. But when asked she had nothing bad to say about the good Pastor... she said he treated her well.'

'Everyone says she left bright and flighty like a butterfly and returned gloomy and bumbly as a moth... at least that's what Aunt Mafiong says.'

'Your father's wife said that?' My aunt stopped and turned toward me, a look of surprise on her face.

'Yes, Aunty.'

'That woman! Isn't she the same person who campaigned for you to replace Ini?'

The silence that accompanied the remains of the journey was broken every now and then by the sound of laborers tapping palm kernels in nearby farms and woodpeckers drilling their way through the hot dry season.

We arrived at the Pastor's place at midday and were given the key to his home by a neighbour.

'Pastor says he'll be back around six... he also said to help yourselves to the jollof rice in the pot with the red lid,' the woman said, handing the keys over to my Aunt.

'Thank you, sister,' my Aunt gave the woman a brief hug. Then she pointed at me. 'This is my niece, she has come to help keep home for Pastor.'

'Eh-yah, welcome, my dear,' the woman turned toward me. 'I am Mama Bomboy... and this is Bom-boy,' she pulled forward a boy of about four years of age. He had been peeping from behind her back since our arrival.

My Aunt threw open the only window to reveal a sparsely furnished but comfortable looking sitting room. There were couches made of burnished and intricately woven cane, complete with a matching centre table. To one side stood a long table made of mahogany wood. Neatly stacked on this were several religious tracts, a brown-covered Bible, and a kerosene lamp. An open corridor led straight to a back door, and there were two closed doors on either side of the corridor, clearly the entrances to the bedrooms.

'You get to have your own private room,' Aunt Emilia said, following my eyes to the door. 'This is good… this is very good,' she said, nodding all the while as if she had personally asked for the room to be made available. To help me settle in, she offered to stay until the Pastor returned.

Pastor Joshua came back three hours later and after some pleasantries between him and my Aunt, I was directed to what was to be my room. I had never owned my own bed, and so the six-spring iron bed complete with foam mattress and a new raffia mat felt like pure luxury. After more polite bantering, interspersed with prayers and words of benediction, my aunt took her to leave.

The first night in my new home was peaceful. Back home, rice meals were enjoyed on special occasions like Christmas and Easter. And now, on my first night here, my stomach was full of well-prepared jollof-rice and smoked mackerel fish. I went to bed thanking God for my good fortune.

Pastor Joshua left the house early the next day. A few hours later he returned with two bundles of plastic bags, one in each hand.

'Prepare stew for lunch with the fresh fish and use the other things to make soup,' he said, handing over the first bag. 'Before you do that, go and try this on,' he said as he passed me the second bag.

I peeked in, and a smile broke over my face. There was a blue dress, complete with matching sandals.

'Thank you very much, Sir Pastor,' I bowed and went in to try on my new gifts. The dress and sandals fit well. I had never owned such a beautiful outfit, and as I came out of the room I still wore a smile on my face.

'Nice! Very nice,' he said, as I twirled enthusiastically for his inspection.

'Thank you, Sir,' I said again, for what seemed like the hundredth time, before walking back to my room to remove the outfit. As I closed the door I caught a look on his face which unsettled me. It was the look I'd seen on the faces of the livestock traders in Ekpa Itak.

A few minutes later I opened the first bag in the kitchen. My mouth widened in surprise. There were foodstuffs in there the likes of which I had never before seen at a single sitting... and for ordinary, everyday cooking – goat meat, dry catfish, fresh fish, even stockfish! A delicacy reserved only for very special occasions and even then, usually one in which important chiefs and elders were present. I went back to the sitting room to thank him.

'No problem, my dear,' he said. 'I want you to be happy here.'

The next day he went out early again. This time he returned with breakfast items – Bournvita, bread, Quaker oats, a tin of powdered peak milk, two tins of sardines, a packet of sugar, and a scarf for me. As with the day before, I thanked him profusely. Again, he responded that he wanted me to be happy there.

The same happened on the third day.

He bought me the best gift of all on the fourth day: a registration form for my entry into secondary school the following September.

That evening, Pastor asked that I stay to sponge his back after I'd readied his bucket of warm water and taken it to the bathroom.

My jaw dropped and I felt my face suffused with heat. I quickly turned away as he casually untied the towel around his waist and hung it over the wall of the shack.

'Nothing to be shy about, Idongesit. Come here, take and soap this,' he handed over a wet sponge and a bar of soap.

My hands shook as I soaped the dripping sponge and ran it up and down his back, avoiding the crack between his buttocks.

'It's finished, Sir' I dropped the sponge in the soap dish and hurried to make my escape.

'No, you haven't,' he said, grabbing my wrist before I could fully turn away. He picked up the sponge, turned and pointed to his chest and belly before handing the sponge to me once again; then, he threw back his head and waited. I began scrubbing, my face turned away in extreme embarrassment and shame.

It happened again the following day. This time, he reprimanded me when I attempted to look away.

'How can you see what you're doing if you don't look?'

And so I did.

'There,' he said, indicating his groin. 'Scrub there,' he nudged my hand downward.

My chest heaved with mortification as I worked the sponge, my fingers becoming tangled in the hair surrounding his manhood.

For the next week I was made to wash him every evening, each time adding another portion of his skin, so that by the end of the sixth day there was not a part of him that I hadn't scrubbed. Now I knew why my cousin would not stay. Within days I too was asking to be returned home.

'Why? Because of a small thing like sponging my back? You think I would ask you if I could reach my back to do it myself? It's normal to ask someone to help if you can't do something yourself. Didn't your father and stepmother teach you that?'

'They did, Sir,' I drew a circle with my big toe. I could not bear to look him in the eyes.

'Then what's the problem here? Surely, your father has asked you to scrub his back before? Oh, wait — of course, he hasn't! That's because your stepmother does it for him,' he said before I could answer, as if the thought had just occurred to him.

He went out early the next day and a few hours later he was back, bearing new gifts – another dress, and a white straw hat with yellow water lilies along the brim.

'These are to thank you for helping sponge my back,' he said. They were beautiful.

'Do you still want to go home?' he asked. I am only scrubbing his body. No one has ever spoken to me about this. Perhaps it's normal. Papa has never asked me, maybe it's because Aunty Mafiong does it for him, as Sir Pastor says, I thought.

'Do you?' the Pastor asked, even more gently, taking my hand and looking deep into my eyes.

'No, Sir Pastor.'

'Good! Now take this, go and prepare lunch,' he said, handing over a brown plastic bag. I looked in: there was rice, some fish, and shank of roasted goat meat. I went off to do as I'd been told.

That night he called me into his room. Before going in, I went to the kitchen and filled his drinking tumbler with water, thinking it was why he needed my attention. He was lying on his bed, naked. I looked down, confused.

'Water? No, no, that's not why I called. Come in. Set the water on that table,' he said, gesturing toward a side table in the far corner of the room. I did as he requested but made no move to go closer.

'Come! Come! And shut the door. I won't bite... I am not a dog.' When I still made no move, he stood up and came to get me.

'No, Sir. I don't want to, Sir, please,' I tried to pull my hand out of his grasp.

'I won't do anything to you. I just want you to sleep here tonight... nothing more.' He pushed me firmly me onto his bed and then lay down beside me. Then, throwing his hands in the air he said,

'See, I'm not touching you. I told you I just want company. Nothing more,' he added, moving away to the far edge of his side of the bed.

I believed him. Slowly, my heart stilled and I fell asleep.

It seemed as if my eyes had only closed for a few minutes when I felt his palm roving up and down my body, and his erect manhood prodding my back. I jerked awake, wide-eyed and afraid.

'Sir Pastor! Please, Sir, what are you doing?' I pushed his hand away and moved as far from him as the wall on my side of the bed would allow.

'Sssshhhh,' was his only response, as he reached out and pulled me back to him. I struggled and begged to be let go, but his finger began to prod places no one had ever touched me before. 'Sssssshhh' he said again. 'I'll be gentle…I p-p-prom-ise it won't hurt,' his voice was raspy and his breath came in stutters.

Clamping my legs and eyes shut, I struggled and began to weep.

'Quiet!' he said. 'You want to wake up the entire compound?'

The more I struggled the more excited he got. Eventually, I felt something warm and sticky between my legs. I gagged at the strange smell.

For the next week, this became the norm. I demanded to be taken home and cried constantly. Then, one day, I threatened to tell the neighbours.

For almost a week he stopped ordering me to his room or asking me to scrub his back. Instead, he took to praying in a very loud voice in the middle of the night. The topic of his prayers was always the casting out of witches and wizards. Sometimes, his prayers were so loud that villagers came to the house and joined in. They never tried to come into the Pastor's home, just gathered around his house chanting loud 'Amens' to the prayers issuing from inside. The light from their kerosene lamps pene-trated the cracks of the wooden window and cast eerie shadows across my room, adding to his bizarre behaviour.

A week later, I was still exhaling a big sigh of relief, believing that my threats had been effective when he came into my room. I guess he knew I would not have obeyed had he summoned me to him. He came while I was asleep and lifted me, kicking and struggling, to his room. I tried to scream but he clamped his palm over my mouth. I bit into it and he jerked back, lifting the same hand and slapping me, hard.

I tasted blood.

'Listen, you little witch, you utter one single word and I'll tell them you're a witch!'

The breath exploded out of me. He saw the fear in my eyes.

'Interested now, are you?' he said, a look of triumph in his eyes. 'From now on you'll do as I say, or I'll tell everyone I've discovered you're a witch and that you're responsible for the inability of your stepmother to conceive.'

'I'll deny it,' I said, my voice breaking even as I mumbled the words.

'Deny?' he laughed mockingly. Raking my shaking body up and down with narrowed eyes he said, 'Who'll believe you? I'm the Pastor; who do you think people will believe, especially after my fervent prayers of the past week?'

He hovered over my trembling body in triumph. Judging by the steeliness in his voice I knew he wasn't joking. The breath left my body.

To be declared a witch was the worst thing that could happen to anyone. I would be ostracized by my community, branded and hounded until I wished fervently for my own death. I had heard about young children being taken from the village and abandoned in the middle of nowhere. No one ever knew what became of them, as no one ever heard of them again. A couple of years before, a young boy in our village had been declared a witch and no one was allowed to play with him. At school, he was seated far away from other children. Everything he did was viewed with suspicion. If he looked at anyone and they happened to develop a fever, he was accused of burning their spirit in the arena of the dark spiritual world; if a market woman passed him on the way to the market, and could later not sell her goods, it was said that he put a curse on her. When our village was visited by inexplicable drought, he was blamed. In short, there was no calamity, natural or otherwise, that would not be attributed to me if I were declared a witch. Above all, what I feared most was that no one would ever share food with me.

Pastor Joshua had the upper hand and he'd played it well.

'Got your attention now, have I?' he mocked again.

'Now, behave yourself!' he ordered. And then he hooked his fingers on my dress, just beneath the nape of my neck, and tore it from the top to the bottom.

I shiver even now at the memory, despite the roaring fire of the stove in my grandmother's kitchen.

Thinking I am catching a cold from the late-November Harmattan air, Grandma Liz leans forward to stoke the fire in the stove some more. Afterward, she turns toward me.

'Here!' she says, nudging me off the little stool. She moves it closer to the fire. 'Now sit!' she orders. I smile my thanks and my thoughts return to the horrors of that time.

For the next six weeks, I laid awake each night trying to anticipate the Pastor's every move. Papa had asked the Pastor to bring me back to visit during the third month of my stay. Counting the days occupied my wakeful hours, while my sleep became intermittent, troubled and feverish. Often, I was too afraid to close my eyes, and when they gave way to exhaustion, nightmares pervaded my sleep. Dreams of dark, threatening beings with giant phalluses chasing me through evil forests and empty houses haunted me. Within weeks, I lost weight so considerably that other tenants in the compound noticed.

'Are you eating, my child? It's home, isn't it? You're missing home?' Mama Bomboy queried.

I longed to confide in her... in someone... anyone, about what was happening, but the Pastor had done his job well. I became more afraid of being labelled a witch than being raped.

So, to every question or query, I simply shook my head and told them I was not ill, that I was eating well; that the Pastor was treating me well; and, yes, that the reason I was looking lean was that I missed my home and family.

'Eeyyaaahh,' Mama Bomboy responded. 'Sorry, my daughter. Don't worry, you'll soon get used to living here. The pastor is a good man. He'll take you to visit with your family soon. Have you asked him?'

'Yes, Mma,' I replied, not knowing what else to say.

The nightly visits persisted. There seemed now to be no hope of it ever ending. If he wasn't going to take me home, I had to make him.

But how? I came up with several ideas and rejected one after another.

And then the idea of suicide lit up like lightning. I wasn't really going to kill myself, I just needed the attempt to look convincing.

I waited till mid-morning the following Saturday when the Pastor and other tenants were at home. Then I took the jar of kerosene we used for cooking out to the courtyard – the common area for all the tenants. Pinching my nostrils to stop me from gagging, I drank the contents. Having refused to eat anything that morning, my empty stomach was ripe for the kind of commotion that ensued within it – commotion I'd prayed would be extreme. It was.

Within minutes I was retching and wailing. Weeks of pent-up frustration spewed out of me as the kerosene burned its way down into my stomach.

The reaction was instantaneous. Tenants poured to my side as I lay heaving and screaming on the ground. They came out of their homes... some half-dressed. Younger children stopped crying and stared, open-mouthed; hens stopped pecking and flew helter-skelter, squawking dramatically. Someone lifted me from the ground, as frantic questions poured from the gathering crowd. The noise brought out the Pastor, who was in his room, writing his sermon in readiness for the following day.

If I hadn't been so consumed by my own misery and pain, the look on his face would have made up for all my months of agony: it was a combination of fear, shock, and more fear.

It wasn't long before everyone understood what had happened – especially with the jar of kerosene lying on its side right where I'd left it, glug-glugging out the last drop onto the sandy earth.

'She drank kerosene! Oh my God! Someone, go get palm oil,' a voice ordered.

'Aloe vera juice is better. Get that! Squeeze the juice into a cup... hurry!'

'But why? Why did she drink kerosene?'

'She misses home; she wanted to be taken home,' another answered.

'Pastor, you have to take her home,' one of the tenants advised. 'This kind of thing is serious.'

'Take her home today,' another added.

'I'll take her home this evening,' he replied in a subdued voice. That was all I needed to hear. It made the liquid fire burning down my chest worthwhile.

Meanwhile, I continued to retch as the oil and juice were poured down my throat.

After the situation had calmed down, the Pastor wheeled his motorcycle from the shed and rode out of the compound. He asked Mama Bom-boy to lend me a hand in packing up my things as I wasn't strong enough to do it myself.

For the rest of that day, the poor woman did not leave my side. When not dripping more oil or aloe vera juice down my throat, she bathed my brow with a piece of torn fabric dipped in warm water.

'My dear child, why? Why?' she repeated every now and again, as she sponged my face with the wet, warm fabric.

Pastor Joshua returned several hours later. After a couple of exchanges with the neighbours – mostly expressions of gratitude for their help earlier that day – and without saying much to me other than 'is your bag packed?' I climbed on to the passenger seat of his motorcycle, making sure to wedge the bag containing my few personal belongings in the middle, between us. I'd left behind every single gift he'd ever bought for me.

He revved the engine, turned the machine around and out we rode from the compound. Despite all that had happened in the past two months, the sense of exhilaration I felt as we retraced the path I'd taken weeks before with my Aunt, is something I cannot put into words. For the first time in my young life, I understood the meaning of the word freedom. The trees and shrubbery along the path danced and bent with the pull of the wind as we sped by. It seemed as though they, even they, were acknowledging the unspoken joy and feeling of liberty flowing inside me.

Free! At last, I am free from this monster, I exulted as we sped through the forest path.

As we turned into the driveway of my family's compound about an hour later, I saw many people gathered around the veranda of our house. As the motorcycle coasted to a stop, I realized that aside from a few close neighbours, most of those present were family members. Wondering why so many of them were there... and looking so sombre, I alighted from the machine and, hoisting the bag with my few personal belongings in one hand, began walking towards my father, who was deep in conversation with some of my uncles. My heart raced. Was someone sick, or dead? Was it Gran-gran? Surely, Papa would have sent a message to me if Grandma Liz were ill; he knows how much she means to me.

I scanned the crowd and offered greetings here and there. To which a few responded; others just avoided my gaze or muttered something under their breath. I was too worried to pay attention to what they were saying.

'Why is she talking like that,' a voice in the crowd whispered – baffled by my raspy voice.

My father made no effort to get up as I walked forward. Instead, he regarded me stealthily and without a smile. Having been gone for almost three months, that alone should have warned me that I was in for trouble.

'Good afternoon, Papa; Good afternoon, my fathers,' I said, turning to address my uncles.

Before any of them could respond, my stepmother streaked from inside the house, behind the door where she must have been hovering. In a second she was upon me screaming and slapping my face left, right, left, right before she was eventually overpowered and pulled away by several of those present.

'What did I ever do to you, eh... I say? What did I ever do to you... you wicked, evil child?' She strained to get at me again.

'Mafiong!' Calm down! Let us approach this thing step by step,' my father said, 'we have questions to ask Idongesit and---'

'Ask her? What questions? What is there to ask her?' my stepmother screamed. 'Will the questions bring back all the babies from my womb she has eaten with her witchcraft? When I think of my kindness toward her... how I have treated her like my own child... unlike some stepmothers in this community, I have treated her with love and care, as if she were my own. Oh, my poor head! To think I've been harbouring a viper in my very bosom? Imagine! All this while my arch enemy was not an outsider but one in my own household...' She continued with both arms on her head, heedless of Papa's and my uncles' continued remonstrations that she be quiet and let them get to the bottom of what they'd been told by Pastor Joshua.

'Ehn...uh...uh?' I muttered stupidly, dumbfounded at the mention of witchcraft. I swiveled in the direction of Pastor Joshua. The smirk on his face chilled my spine and plunged me into a panic. Without a second thought, I turned... and began to run.

I will never know what caused me to take that mindless step. I supposed people react to calamities differently and, often, in an extremely weird and bizarre fashion. All I know is that that single action sealed my fate. In the eyes of those present, running could only mean one thing: I was guilty of what was being levelled against me.

And all of those present, except my Aunt Emilia, treated me as one would a guilty person. Her tearful 'Senior brother, please let us hear what Idongesit has to say,' was drowned out by the barrage of angry voices.

'Devil.'

'Daughter of Satan.'

'Merciless excuse for a child! All these years, her own father—imagine! To think she's responsible for the poor man's anguish... may God deliver us from evil children like her.' 'Wicked soul. See her crying... pretender. Bring her here... let her confess her evil.' These were lashed out without pity, as those nearest caught and dragged me towards my father and uncles.

'Papa... he's lying. He touched me, Papa... he's lying.' I whispered, my throat still hoarse.

'Speak up! What's wrong with your voice?' one of my uncles demanded, watching me struggle to free myself from the grasp of my captors.

But I could not.

Suddenly overwhelmed by emotion, I went mute. Everything became quiet... or so it seemed. The accusing faces before me swum in and out of focus. I felt as if I were in a glass jar, seeing but barely hearing what they were saying. 'Why, Idongesit? Who taught this evil to you? Who initiated you into the secrets of the dark?' I heard my father say brokenly.

He doesn't believe me, I thought, casting my eyes to where Pastor Joshua was standing. His permanent expression of surprise lent him an air of what others saw as innocence. Of course, I knew he was gloating.

It was rare to see men cry in our community. My father turned his back and wiped his eyes. No man cried in our community.

Pulling free at last from my captors, I threw myself at his feet and wept.

Unknown to me, when the Pastor left earlier that morning he had visited my family and told them that God had revealed to him that I was a witch. He explained that when he had tried, in the course of one week of prayer and fasting, to exorcize the evil spirit from me I had snarled and barked at him like a dog. At first, my family had not believed him until he told them that the people in his village could testify to the fasting and prayers he was referring to because they themselves joined in on several occasions.

When the furore had subsided and I was finally allowed to tell my side of the story, very few people believed me.

'He said it! The good Pastor said that she threatened to accuse him of molesting her if he exposed her evil deeds,' my stepmother rolled her eyes towards the heavens as if she could not quite believe my father's naivety.

'She's still my daughter and—' Papa began.

'Your daughter! Is that all you have to say? What about me? You don't care that your precious daughter is a witch? That she is the cause of all my pain?'

The next few days under my father's roof became unbearable. My usually talkative Papa became quiet and took to staying in his room. My stepmother wanted absolutely nothing to do with me. She was hard-pressed to even feed me and when she did, out of consideration for my father, she would dish the food into the dirtiest bowl she could find and fling it at me saying, 'There! Eat so you can have the strength to further destroy my life!'

It mattered little to me whether or not I was fed, anyway. All I wanted was to be left alone... and preferably to die; but until death came along, I just wanted to be left alone.

My grandmother learned of the incident and arrived the following day. She, of course, did not believe the allegations. But she was the lone voice in the sea of those who would have me condemned. Knowing what awaited me, she insisted that my father allow her to take me back with her to her village. My father refused, at first. And so she left, promising to come back in two days.

The only other person who would have had an inkling of what happened was Ini, the cousin who had first gone to serve Pastor Joshua. But the fear of also being declared a witch was too great for her to speak about it. She was her mother's only child and could not afford to be tarred with the stigma of witchcraft. She later admitted privately to me that she was also afraid that people would find out she was no longer a virgin, and that Pastor Joshua's abuse would jeopardize her chance of ever marrying well.

I was alone... an outcast. My innocence was stolen. My childhood destroyed. My future eclipsed. And unless something happened to counter the Pastor's accusations, so it would remain. Even at an age where I did not fully comprehend the attending meaning of the word, future, the prospect of being an outcast for life was terrifying.

Meanwhile, my life became a nightmare. Women rained curses on me wherever I went and children followed, taunting me and chanting, 'Witch, witch, eater of unborn babies; witch, witch, drinker of innocent blood!'

About a week later, my father finally realised that his roof was no longer a safe place for me. My stepmother had just finished her meal and without clearing up, left the kitchen area in the courtyard to go into the main house. In an effort to help, I began picking up the crumbs of cassava and chewed fish bones littering the spot where she had sat to take her meal.

'Ehn, what are doing? What's that in your hand?' I heard her yell behind my back. Before I could react or turn around, she had rushed forward and forced open my closed palm.

One of the beliefs about witchcraft practices is that those who possess the secrets of the dark pick up the after-dinner crumbs from the tables of those they wish to curse and use them in spells to impoverish the person who had eaten the meal.

'Hey! People of Ikot Eda, come! Come and witness my calamity at the hands of this heartless child. She's not satisfied with destroying my unborn babies, now she wants to beggar me as well.' She leaned down, grabbing a piece of wood still smouldering in the kitchen stove. Rounding on me, she hit me across the back with it.

I smelled my own flesh burning as the hot coal laid a path of searing pain on my upper back. Ours was a close-knit community of sprawling huts and houses, with no fence or gate separating one house from another. My stepmother's screams were heard all across the village. As I lay writhing on the ground, people poured in from every direction. While some castigated my step-mother for having gone too far, others hissed that I deserved what I was getting.

The next day, my father delivered me to Grandma Liz's house.

'You'll be safer here,' he said, before pedalling out of the compound on his old bike.

'Pass me that knife, the one on top of the red plate,' Grandma Liz interrupts my thoughts, pointing at a kitchen knife with a black wooden handle. I pick up the knife and hand it to her.

While I had been steeped in my memories, she had finished picking and washing the greens. She lays a big piece of cut wood in an enamel tray. Taking a handful of leaves, she squeezes them to get rid of the excess water and breaks the bunch in two. Then she lay this across the cutting stick and slices them in long, thin strips. As the knife crunch-crunches through the bundle of greens in her hands, my mind goes back to that fateful time.

Although life in my grandmother's village was nowhere near as bad as it had been in my father's village, the news that I was a witch had travelled fast. I was given a wide berth by adults and children alike. No one wanted to be friends with me, nor was I welcome to interact with other children. Grandma's garri business also began to suffer, as most of her customers stopped buying from her. No one wanted to buy a ready-to-eat staple from a household that was harbouring a witch. Fear of the food being tainted by witchcraft and their being unknowingly initiated into that most-feared of cults was all too prevalent. As that was my grandma's only livelihood, our situation worsened rapidly. She sent a message to her brother, asking that I be allowed to live with him and his family in Onitsha, but he sent back word that his two-bedroom apartment was already too small for him, his wife, and their four children, and that it was not going to be convenient to take in an extra person. Instead, he offered to contribute financially to any alternative plan Grandma Liz could come up with. My grandma and I knew that it was just an excuse. Obviously, my uncle's wife had baulked at the idea of welcoming a proclaimed witch into her household.

Even though she could scarcely afford to care for herself, Grandma Liz decided to send me to board at a Catholic mission school some fifty kilometers from her village.

'Nne, the cost! How will we afford that,' I protested.

'My brother, your uncle, will help. Even if he doesn't, I am prepared to sell the last wrapper on my waist to restore a semblance of the future that has been stolen from you.'

Filled with gratitude, I threw myself into her embrace.

'God will make a way for us; don't you worry, Idongesit-mi' she said. 'Don't you worry,' she repeated, running her palm up and down my back.

I had, of course, narrated everything that had happened after which she confronted my father, demanding to know what he was going to do about it. But he could do nothing because my stepmother was convinced I was lying. According to her, my accusation was a ruse to confuse everyone and remove focus from the 'real issue.' Aside from that, Pastor Joshua was so renowned for his acts of charity and 'integrity' that it was easier to believe him than me.

To be sure, it was said that some people in our village had begun to question his accusations, but they were very few voices of reason. Moreover, there were two indisputable 'facts' stacked against me, some said. One was my stepmother's inexplicable miscarriages - which the Pastor insisted was the first revelation he'd had that I was a witch. The second, and most damning, was the fact that I had tried to run away. As far as most were concerned, that was a glaring indication of my guilt.

'Here, wash your hands,' Grandma Liz says, her voice cutting once more into my reminiscence. 'Soup will be ready in a minute.' She pushes a plastic basin towards me, into which she pours some water. As I wash my hands, she takes another plate – a flat silver one this time – and uncovering a deep plastic bowl standing by her side, she reaches in and cuts out a big portion of fufu and begins to knead it in the silver plate until it is smooth. Then she pats it down, forming a smooth round lump.

Three months after Papa delivered me to Grandma Liz, I left for boarding school.

'See you in March,' my Grandma said.

'Okay,' I mumbled reluctantly. Although I was sad to leave my grandmother, I had no idea what my welcome would be like when I returned to the village, so I did not look forward to returning during the holidays.

Two years later Pastor Joshua struck again.

This time the girl was fourteen years old. She became pregnant. The Pastor tried to have the baby aborted. The girl bled out... and died.

When the story erupted, the father of the girl went after Pastor Joshua with a sharpened cutlass. Luckily for the Pastor, the bereaved man was stopped.

Still, the Council of Chiefs of their village agreed that the Pastor's crime demanded swift justice.

Grandma Liz told me what happened to him when I went home on holiday. 'He was stripped naked. They covered him in ground charcoal and paraded him around the whole village... and around the square of their big market – in full view of everyone. It was during that process that they said a woman called Mama Bom-boy – I believe you know her– asked that he be made to tell the real truth behind your accusation. Faced with growing hostility from the villagers, the Pastor confessed. A few days later he left the village in the middle of the night. No one has seen him since or knows where he has disappeared to. He is now an outcast. You've been vindicated. Justice has been done,' she nodded sagely, her face suffused with deep contentment.

'Tomorrow is the beginning of a beautiful new start for you,' she says now. 'You have no need to live in fear, anymore, Adia-ha-ima. Justice is done... you are free,' she nods, repeating the same words she had said to me so many years ago.

I know she is right. Pastor Joshua was eventually exposed for the fraud and monster that he was; He is now the outcast, not me. I know that my father and stepmother, and all who were involved in my suffering, have begged my forgiveness. I know that justice eventually prevailed. But it happened at a huge price. It took the destruction of three innocent lives, and possibly countless others, before people saw sense. It seems to me that justice always shows up in the end, but only after the innocents have suffered. I can't explain this to Grandma Liz. She thinks that I should be able to put it all behind me. She looks at me, as if she wants to say something.

Instead, she pushes the steaming bowl of vegetable soup toward me. 'Eat!' she says, and ruffles my hair.

'*Ekong nke-e.*'

'*Nke ekong Abasi,*' Esit-Ima bows her head as she responds to the now familiar chant. 'Nana, there is so much in this story: witchcraft, rape, broken trust, poverty, inequality, superstition, ignorance...'

'That's right, my heart. And it's because life happens within tangles of connected and interconnected issues, not in a vacuum or isolation.'

'It's a terrible thing when a mother dies and leaves behind her children, isn't it?'

'A terrible thing indeed, my heart.'

'And poverty, Nana, being poor is a terrible thing. Wealth to me is not really about having the money to buy big houses and fancy, expensive cars. Wealth is being able to eat, have a roof over one's head, clothes to cover one's nakedness, and enough to be able to give one's children an education... a good education.'

The old woman fixes her eyes on her granddaughter. There is a flicker of surprise in those eyes. 'Is that how you view wealth, Koko-Ima?'

'Yes, it is, Nana. I would like to become rich, very rich, please know that, Nana. But if I never have more than those very basic things, I will consider life sweet, and successful.'

'Then hold onto that, Koko-nmi. Hold onto that deeply. Let that become one of the essential tools in your toolbox of life.' The old woman nods sagely, a soft smile playing around her lips. There is a faraway look in her eyes even though she is fixing them steadily on Esit-Ima.

'Why, Nana? Why does my answer please you?'

126

'Not naming big cars and fine houses as your first idea of what makes for wealth, that pleases me. It tells me your head is properly placed on your neck. It pleases me, my heart.'

Esit-Ima thinks about what her Nana has just spoken for a while, then changing the topic completely she says, 'This issue of witchcraft, Nana. It is an easy accusation for anyone to make. It has been used so many times, not only by fake spiritual leaders, to destroy so many homes, so many lives.'

'I know. That's because many people are fearful and ignorance. It's a way of exploiting this ignorance and fear. Education is the only way to eradicate a belief in witchcraft.'

'Idong-esit...how she suffered, Nana! To be so isolated. To have her own family turn against her. And she is right, justice does always seem to show up only after the innocents have suffered greatly.'

'This story has made you sad, my heart, hasn't it?'

'Yes, Nana, it has.'

'In that case, let me tell you another one. The first leg of your marriage starts tomorrow. I want you in good humour, my heart.'

'*Ekong nke-e.*'

'*Nke ekong Abasi, ekong aka, ekong oyong, ekon isi maha udim.*'

Good Tidings

TAILOR Timothy's heartbeat accelerated and his heart pounded as he spied the rooftops of *Ukana* some distance away. He stumbled as his foot hit a stump on the bush path. The pain raced like bushfire up his leg and embedded itself in a part of his brain he hadn't even known existed. He dropped on all fours on the hard, dusty ground. Some soldier ants that were bustling back and forth a few inches from his face stopped for a moment, then scattered in all directions, as if terrified by the huge dark face looming above them with its bared teeth.

Timothy threw his head back and grimaced as the pain continued to slither around in his brain. More than anything else, it seemed to signify the hopelessness of the task ahead of him.

Timothy tottered back upright on his feet. The nail of the big toe hung loose like a partly opened can of sardines. Blood oozed from underneath it and puddled on the ground.

'Great! Now I am arriving with the smell of blood already in the air,' he muttered. He looked ahead and saw smoke billowing from the roofs of some of the houses. The grey, foamy matter spiraled upward and disappeared into the increasingly dark sky.

Stubbing my toe probably won't be the worst thing that will happen to me tonight, he thought, before hobbling forward

His village, Ikot Esin, had received an *Ayei*[1] from the Paramount Ruler of Ukana. The Paramount Ruler's heir was missing and the village of Ukana believed that someone in Timothy's village knew something about it. This is because a piece of the boy's clothing had been found in Ikot Esin. When he found out why the *Ayei* had been sent, Timothy had reacted with something approaching panic. *Ayei* was a declaration of war.

He remembered how his hands had shook as he tried to concentrate on his work. The kaftan he was sewing had slipped from his hands and landed in a heap on the floor. His wife of twenty-four years reached down, picked it up and shook *frap, frap, frap* to get rid of the dust on the cuffs.

'I know we should all be concerned, but you are taking this news particularly hard, husband.'

If she only knew, Timothy thought.

Besides his personal stake in the matter, their village could not afford any enmity with their neighbour. They were a peace-loving people, and besides, they numbered only three thousand compared to the ten thousand in Ukana. Timothy remembered a far-off dispute with Ukana that had led to the death of his father, his eldest brother, and many able-bodied men in their village when he was just a toddler; the horrors of that conflict were still whispered about in some circles. It wasn't for nothing that the village of Ikot Esin had worked hard to co-exist in peace with the Ukanas, despite the latter's tendency toward trouble making.

Peace was on the brink of disappearing now.

'A piece of the boy's clothing found near our village does

1. *Ayei* – an intricately woven fanlike symbol made from fresh palm fronds

not automatically mean our village is responsible for his disappearance. Surely, they can't be that unreasonable,' his wife had leaned forward and touched his hand.

'You're forgetting something. The boy is Paramount Ruler Ibiere's son. They will dig up every available earth in this village, look under the smallest rock, and peel apart every leaf.'

'And so what? Let them dig out the revered remains of our forefathers if they want. What can they find if there's nothing to find?'

Timothy looked at his wife. It was okay for her to argue thus... she did not know what Timothy knew.

Despite her attempt at reassurance, Timothy's mind pictured the image his own words had painted.

That was what scared him the most, the thoroughness of the search about to come. Whatever was in their village would have remained a secret but Ukana would leave no stone unturned.

Had his daughter been right? Had she been telling the truth, after all?

'Papa, I just saw a strange man kill and bury a young boy of about fifteen in the dense undergrowth by the river,' she had declared three weeks before.

'Really, *Nene-Eyen*[2]! A murder no less?' Timothy had replied in the indulgent tone he had come to adopt when he heard his only child's myriad stories.

'I saw it, Papa! With my own two *korokoro* eyes, I did!'[3]

'You did? And the *murderer* of this poor young man allowed such a juicy witness to his heinous crime escape? Mmmm, not

---

2. *Nene-Eyen* (beloved, treasured, most precious): a terms of endearment used by both parents for daughters
3. *Korokoro* – clear, unadulterated.

much of a murderer now, was he? What could he have been thinking of?' Timothy tapped on his nose with one finger.

'He didn't see me, Papa. I hid. He didn't see me.'

'Mmmmm,' Timothy muttered. 'By the way, what of the friends who went with you to the river, did they also witness this horrific crime?'

'I was on my own. Martha and Susanna didn't want to come.'

'You went to the river by yourself? How many times have your mother and I told you not to do that? You see what disobedience does? Had my beloved daughter listened to us she would not have been confronted with such a horrific scene.' Despite his mock attempt at seriousness, Timothy's voice cracked, and he couldn't hold back his laughter.

'You don't believe me? I did, too! I saw! I saw!' his daughter stamped her feet, causing the water she was carrying to slush over the sides of the pail and splatter on the ground.

'Go, put the water down and have something to eat, Nene[4]. Your mother made your dinner before leaving for the market. It's in the blue enamel bowl in the kitchen.'

His daughter opened her mouth to argue then thought better of it. Instead, the thirteen-year-old marched toward the courtyard, a large scowl of disapproval on her cherubic face.

Timothy had stared at the disappearing back, shook his head in amusement before continuing with what he was doing. He'd thought that was the end of it. But the next day she was at it again. But he hadn't believed her. And for good reason.

---

4. *Nene* – beloved, grandmother – a term given to a daughter as mark of honour to one's grandmother

His daughter was a liar and a gossip; the most incurable any-one in the village had ever known. Her loose mouth had caused him and his wife no end of trouble. It had, in fact, got to a point where most felt rather sorry for them.

Her weakness for story-telling did not make them love her any less. But as she grew, they had become increasingly ashamed of her propensity for trouble-making. Timothy often secretly wished he could lock her away. Love her, yes, he and his wife always would, but for her own good, Timothy knew he would willingly incarcerate his daughter... even for a short time. Such an admission, even though never spoken out loud, made his heart bleed, for if his wife adored their daughter, Timothy posi-tively worshipped her. His daughter knew that. His were there-fore the first ears into which she invariably poured her stories.

Timothy could not help the heart-wrenching love he felt for her. She had come to him after more than seventeen years of childlessness – seventeen years of pitying looks, of insinuations that perhaps he, Timothy, wasn't so fertile, after all. His first wife had left in frustration after seven years without a hint of preg-nancy. The humiliation had been great; a child, after all, was a man's way of proving his manhood, of letting the world know that he was indeed a man. He had met his second wife after another three years of self-questioning. She wasn't a great beauty, but Timothy hadn't minded. Having a woman who was ready to stay with him despite the very high possibility that he would never be able to give her children was prize enough. His joy was there-fore stupendous when she became pregnant after eleven years. The daughter that was born was the most beautiful anyone had ever seen... everyone for miles agreed without exception.

In their region a name was not something one gave to a child in a *hula-hoppy* fashion. It had to mean something. It had to be a prayer. It had to be a wish for the kind of future the family wanted for the child. But most especially, it had to express the heart of the parents. And so Timothy thought, what better name to give his daughter than...

Good-Tidings.

His wife agreed.

As *Good-Tidings* grew, so too did her beauty.

'The most saintly face we've ever seen on any but angels,' even the most cynical readily agreed.

'Those big round eyes!'

'Those pouty-red lips'

'That button-nose'

'The full head of inky-black hair on one so young!'

And then *Good-Tidings* turned three; and Timothy and his wife noticed something unusual in their little girl.

'Jonah pinched me on the hand and so much blood poured out.'

The parents panicked, checked her arm. No blood. Checked everywhere else, no discernible blood or fluid of any kind.

'Ini stole my pack of crayons.'

'The cat climbed on the desk and knocked Papa's radio onto the ground, it is broken into many pieces!'

'Theresa says Mama is a wicked woman. She says she hates Mama.' Theresa was his wife's younger sister who lived with them. Her closeness to his wife was unquestionable.

At first his daughter's many fibs were regarded as comic relief, the cause of many evenings of indulgent-head shaking and giggles.

But as she grew they gathered momentum.

The most damning gossip *Good-Tidings* ever uttered was when she was seven. She calmly told everyone she had seen the young wife of their Chief enter the private rooms of a young, unmarried man in the village known for his philandering ways.

'Saw with my own *korokoro* eyes. She came out with only a piece of wrapper across her breast. She looked this way, that way, and then took the secret path behind Uko's place to return home.'

'This is a serious matter *Nene-Eyen*. Are you absolutely sure?' her father asked, looking into the angelic eyes of his daughter for any sign of hesitation.

His daughter stuck out her tongue, touched the tip with her index finger and raised the finger to the sky.

'By the moon and the stars do I swear!' she said.

The Chief was not amused. The young man was hounded out of the village. The Chief's young wife was sent away in disgrace, despite her protestation of innocence. Three months later, when it became obvious the young woman was pregnant, the matter took another turn, with the Chief threatening to butcher the young man if he should ever set foot again in the village again.

Throughout the storm, *Good-Tidings* maintained her stance.

'I saw her with my own two *korokoro* eyes,' she insisted. Bringing her index and middle finger together, she waved them back and forth some inches from her eyes to make her point.

Because she was so young many believed her.

'Such a young child could never tell a lie of such proportion. She must have seen what she says she saw,' an elderly uncle of the Chief said.

And then the Chief's young wife gave birth.

'Like the Chief himself peeled off his skin and attached it on the baby. Never saw such stark resemblance in all my life,' many said.

The Chief took the child but none could convince him to take back his young wife.

The Chief's was not the only havoc-wreaking incidence his daughter's weakness caused over the years.

'Mmmm,' Timothy had exhaled as he remembered.

'No one in this village is foolish enough to mess with Ukana. Whatever happened to the boy must have taken place far, far away from here.' His wife's voice came to him as if from a distance. Her tone did not mirror the same level of panic in his voice.

Yes, but what if their blood-thirsty neighbour believed someone in Ikot Esin had witnessed the murder of their ruler's son and then kept silent? Timothy thought.

And then there was the one law for which Ukana was well known.

Their unshakable belief in *'an eye for an eye.'*

If ten of theirs were killed in any entanglement, the Ukanas would only agree to a settlement or a negotiation of any kind after ten people from the other side were killed. Theirs was An Absolute Law.

Timothy had shivered afresh at the full implication of the *Ayei.*

There was no doubt which side would come out the victor in a war with between Ukana and Ikot Esin.

How was he to break the news to the Chief that his daughter had most probably witnessed the killing of the missing boy?

Timothy no longer doubted that his daughter had witnessed a murder. He had been to the spot that she told of. Even with the dry leaves scattered over it, he had noticed a mound of fresh earth underneath the leaves. The mound was covering the missing boy. The question was how to convince their neighbour that Ikot Esin had no hand in it, or that they had not deliberately concealed the murder of one of Ukana's heirs apparent.

If none in your village is guilty why did you not inform us when you first received this information? The Paramount Ruler of Ukana was sure to ask their Chief. Witnessing a murder is, after all, not something one makes light of.

Many in his community would understand why Timothy hadn't believed his daughter. But when it came to sending a sacrificial lamb, would they consider the fact that his refusal to believe her was valid? Moreover, his daughter had caused so much pain to so many with her loose tongue, who would not want her gone?

That was what scared Timothy the most. His daughter's life was at stake. The one thing in life that validates his existence was about to be snatched away from him.

His fears were given credence when he visited the Chief of his own village two days before.

'You mean you heard something like this and you didn't think to inform us, even knowing the character of the people involved? Chief Usoro's face had darkened in anger.

'Obong mi[5] You know my daughter. And knowing that... how could I?'

5. *Obong mi* – My Lord (origin: southern Nigeria – the Akwa Ibom/Calabar people

'Mmmm. Go home, tailor! I'll call a meeting of the Council of Chiefs. We'll inform you of the outcome.'

Timothy had indeed returned home. But home had ceased to be home. Every time he looked at his daughter his heart contracted. It did not help matters when the young girl began to boast.

'Told you, Papa! Told you I saw a young boy being murdered and then buried!'

'Sssshhh,' his wife rushed forward and covered their daughter's mouth with the opened palm of one hand.

'What's she talking about?' she turned to Timothy, her voice cracking.

'Oh, nothing… don't give a thought to that, you know how she is,' Timothy replied with a flippant toss of hand. His wife looked at him deeply for a moment before turning to 'shush' their daughter once more.

That was four days ago. During that time he had paced back and forth, sleepless through the nights, wondering what to do. And then he had arrived at a solution. Not the greatest, but the best there was under the circumstances.

'You're going to Ntipo… in the state that you are in? Can't you go another time?' His wife's eyebrow squirreled up to her hairline.

'This needs to be done now,' Timothy turned his back on his wife. He could not bear looking into her trusting eyes. He had told her that he was visiting his only sister to settle a quarrel between her and her husband. In truth, he was heading for Ukana.

Perhaps Paramount Ruler Ibiere would have mercy if he stepped forward before his son's body was found under the mound by the river? Timothy could only hope.

'What time should we expect you back?'

'You know how these things go. It will probably take all night. So, I won't be back until tomorrow.'

He was going to plead his case. And if, after hearing what he had to say, the people of Ukana decided to exact their *revenge* at least it would be his life, and not the life of his only child.

He rounded the last corner and the lights and lanterns of the village of Ukana twinkled before him.

Two hours later he was manacled and locked up in a dark, empty mud hut.

The next day, while the sounds of women visiting the streams could be heard through all the surrounding villages, Timothy was brought out and led in a procession towards the burial spot by the river. The Paramount Ruler and the Chiefs encircling him were dressed in their war regalia: wrappers made of cowhide, eagle feathers around their waists and elaborate feathered necklaces. Their traditional caps were also festooned with feathers. Around his waist each man wore a long cutlass sheathed in brown leather cowhide. The face, chest and stomach of each warrior were decorated with white clay and red ochre. Much of the decoration depicted skulls and birds of prey. The entire assembly was a fearful sight to behold. Timothy's stomach was turning over.

That he was not summarily executed was a miracle, but Timothy could not count on staying alive for long. Already the Chief of his village and his council of elders had been sent for.

News of what he had done had reached his village. The sound of his wife and daughter's wails reached him even before Timothy and the Paramount Ruler Ibiere, along with his own Council of Chiefs arrived at the site of the suspicious mound. The road along the river thronged with people from all the surrounding villages, not only Ukana and Ikot Esin.

His wife and daughter were held firmly by three men from his village. Timothy's stomach did another flip at the sight of his daughter. *God of my dead ancestors, let her not make the situation worse. For once, please let her keep her mouth shut.*

His wife tore from the men's grip, rushed forward and threw herself at the feet of the feather-bedecked figure of Paramount Ruler Ibiere.

'Please, Your Highness... Please! Please! Please don't kill him.'

The Paramount Ruler looked at her coldly and shooed her away with his foot. Then he turned to four hefty young men with shovels behind him.

'Dig!' he commanded.

He didn't even acknowledge Chief Usoro, or any of the elders standing around him.

The *thud, plod, thud, plod* lasted less than five minutes before the smell hit them.

The Paramount Ruler reeled. The diggers stopped in reverence to the obvious pain on the face of their Ruler. One of the elders in his council stepped forward to lay a protective hand on him.

The Paramount Ruler brushed the hand aside roughly. Instead, he turned a face of voracious hatred on the manacled Timothy.

'Dig!' he commanded again without taking his eyes off his captive.

The four men dug for a couple more minutes, then they reached down and pulled out the body.

It was covered in a green plastic, the kind used to cover goods on the back of a motorcycle.

The four men pulled the covering aside solemnly. The Paramount Ruler and his Chiefs stepped forward and looked down at the body.

A big sigh cut through the men. Timothy looked down, expecting his life to end any moment as the axe, cutlass, or whatever was going to be used, fell.

'This is not my son,' he heard the utterance as if from a long way. His wife's wailing stopped, like a tap had been turned off. The quiet was deafening.

'This is not my son,' Timothy heard the Paramount Ruler again. At the same time he felt the manacles on his arms loosen. He looked up to see the Paramount Ruler of Ukana step forward and offer his hand to Timothy's Chief.

'It is apparent that something terrible has come into our region. Will you join hands with me to rout out the person responsible?'

Timothy saw Chief Usoro nod many times.

The Paramount Ruler then turned to Timothy.

'My people and I apologize for the indignity we've put you through. Now, can your daughter help us catch this killer? Will she remember enough to describe him to us?'

Timothy got slowly to his feet and took the hand of friendship the Paramount Ruler of *Ukana* was offering. Even though he ought to be troubled afresh at the realization that someone out there was kidnapping and murdering children, his heart bubbled with happiness. The Paramount Ruler was on their side. And Timothy was in no doubt, whoever had kidnapped the voracious clan head's son had picked the wrong victim.

'Yes, Your Highness, I believe she will,' he said. Then turning, he beckoned to his daughter. A few seconds later, Timothy took his little girl's hand proudly.

'Your Royal Highness may I, please, present my lovely daughter, Good-Tidings,' he said.

'*Ekong nke-e.*'

'*Nke ekong Abasi,* Nana. Another beautiful story. Good Tidings, indeed! There is something beautiful in every person, Nana, isn't there?' Esit-Ima is laughing as she says this.

'There certainly is, my heart. And I want you to remember that as Benjie is formally recognized as your life partner to-be tomorrow. I know that you love this boy, and that he certainly loves you too, from what I have seen. I would not have agreed to this union if I wasn't sure of that. Still, there will be moments when that love will be tested. It helps to remember that there is good in everyone, despite whatever weaknesses they might display. It also helps to start this journey with a sense of humour. Like oil to a lamp during the dark is humour to marriage. Let your marriage be saturated with it, find something to laugh about...even if it means directing that laughter at yourself. Infuse your daily actions with comedy. Don't take yourself too seriously. Above all, put God in all that you do and pray.'

'A parent's love is a beautiful thing, Nana. I wonder how I would have related to Good Tidings if she were my own child.'

'A parent's love is indeed a beautiful thing, Koko-Ima; the love of a good parent, it is like refreshing, thunderous rain after years and years of drought.'

'*Ekong nke-e.*'

'*Nke ekong Abasi, ekong aka, ekong oyong, ekong isi maha udim.*'

About the Author

Sarah Udoh-Grossfurthner is a Nigerian-born writer and poet whose work covers the highs and lows of the human heart. Her writings include *BUT HE CALLS ME BLESSED! When the Unbelievable Happens to Believers* – the widely reviewed non-fiction on the true life stories of five different women, and the awe-inspiring faith that saw them beating odds that would brought most to their knees, *Pathways of Life*, her 2008 book of poetry, *Just An Ordinary Guy*, *The Heavens also Weep* (shortlisted in the Wasafiri Prize, 2017) and features in *TIME* magazine, and numerous others in *Genevieve Lifestyle Magazine*, *Leadership & Life Style monthly*, and many other publications. She is also the co-editor of (and contributor in) *Payback and Other Stories: An Anthology of African and African Diaspora Short Stories* (spearheaded by Prof. Dr. Adams Bodomo, Professor of African Studies (Chair of Languages and Literatures), University of Vienna, African Studies Department). Born in Southern Nigeria, Sarah's poem "Mirror Image" was converted into the theme song for a Nigerian breast cancer awareness concert in 2005. She holds a Bachelor's in Diplomatic Studies and a Master's in Professional Writing from the University College of Falmouth, Cornwall. She is blessed with two children and currently lives and writes in Vienna.

For more information, please visit:
www.sarahudohgrossfurthner.com.

Printed in Poland
by Amazon Fulfillment
Poland Sp. z o.o., Wrocław